"There's Think this through."

Tommy underestimated her need to escape. Cassi shrugged, appearing flippant, but in truth she was stalling, waiting for the strength to return to her limbs. She was starting to think that's why he'd tackled her then stayed on top of her, to weaken her. Well, if it was, it had worked and it'd also destroyed her hope that he'd stayed put simply because he liked being there. *There's a blow to the ol' ego.* She flexed her fingers and gave him a hard look of her own.

"Sorry, Tommy. I can't. There's no way I can make you understand, and that's a tragedy. But I'm not going anywhere with you. That man killed my mother and I'm going to prove it somehow. It's the only chance I have of making things right. So if you want to take me in...you'll have to kill me first."

Dear Reader,

This book kicks off an exciting new series entitled Mama Jo's Boys. Mama Jo, a foster mother with a heart big enough to fit three boys who aren't of her blood but are hers just the same, connects each book, and she's a wonderful character. We could all benefit from having a "Mama Jo" in our lives.

The first book features Thomas Bristol and Cassi Nolan, true soul mates who found each other in childhood, but along the way to adulthood, lost sight of what was important. I confess, I love stories like this. I think there is something magical and pure about first love, and those who are lucky enough to hold on to that love are truly blessed.

The second book features Christian Holt and Skye D'Lane, two people in the Big Apple trying to make things right in their world and finding love along the way.

The trilogy ends with Owen Garrett and Piper Sunday and I think you're going to find these two quite entertaining as they fight their attraction to one another while they uncover a twenty-five-year-old secret within their California town.

In all, Mama Jo's Boys are hot, sexy, strong men with eyes only for the one woman who can drive them crazy but at the same time, make them fall madly in love.

Hearing from readers is one of my greatest joys (aside from really good chocolate) so don't be shy. Feel free to drop me a line at my website www.kimberlyvanmeter.com or through snail mail: P.O. Box 2210, Oakdale, CA 95361.

Happy reading,

Kimberly Van Meter

The Past Between Us

Kimberly Van Meter

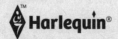

TORONTO NEW YORK LONDON
AMSTERDAM PARIS SYDNEY HAMBURG
STOCKHOLM ATHENS TOKYO MILAN MADRID
PRAGUE WARSAW BUDAPEST AUCKLAND

Recycling programs
for this product may
not exist in your area.

ISBN-13: 978-0-373-71694-4

THE PAST BETWEEN US

Copyright © 2011 by Kimberly Sheetz

ABOUT THE AUTHOR

Kimberly Van Meter wrote her first book at age sixteen and finally achieved publication in December 2006. She writes for Harlequin Superromance and Silhouette Romantic Suspense. She and her husband of seventeen years have three children, three cats and always a houseful of friends, family and fun.

Books by Kimberly Van Meter

HARLEQUIN SUPERROMANCE

1391—THE TRUTH ABOUT FAMILY
1433—FATHER MATERIAL*
1469—RETURN TO EMMETT'S MILL*
1485—A KISS TO REMEMBER*
1513—AN IMPERFECT MATCH*
1577—KIDS ON THE DOORSTEP*
1600—A MAN WORTH LOVING*
1627—TRUSTING THE BODYGUARD*

*Home in Emmett's Mill

SILHOUETTE ROMANTIC SUSPENSE

1622—TO CATCH A KILLER
1638—GUARDING THE SOCIALITE

To fellow Silhouette author Susan Crosby,
a woman of quiet wisdom and gentle humor.
Not only is she an inspiration and a joy,
she reminds me with the patience of someone
who has already "been there, done that"
what remains important, whether it's advice
applied to career or personal issues.
I don't know what I'd do
without our bi-monthly chats!

To my family, for—*always, always,
always*—being my biggest fans!
From yelling the loudest at my various
graduations to telling every single person they
come into contact with about my books...
I would be nothing without you!

Lastly, to my editor, Johanna,
and agent, Pam—two ladies whose
vision and insight never fail to steer me
in the right direction. Thank you!

CHAPTER ONE

WARM MOISTURE TRICKLED between the valley of her breasts, which were bound tightly by the purple sports bra she'd found at a little thrift store on Third. Her muscles were loose and slack from the workout, and she mentally congratulated herself for managing to convince a class of twenty upwardly mobile New York executive-types that she'd been teaching yoga for the past six years when in fact, she'd only just assumed this identity in the past month. She dabbed a thin towel at her hairline and slung it around her neck. This was by far the easiest identity she'd ever taken on and she actually liked being Trinity Moon, the earthy yoga instructor who believed in peace and love, vegan food and karma.

She really liked the karma part. If karma really worked, she enjoyed imagining that her stepfather was destined to be reincarnated as a dung beetle. Although, that was probably unfair to all the industrious dung beetles on the earth who were not nearly as odious as Lionel Vissher.

Unpleasant memories blotted out her previous

feel-good, exercise-induced endorphins and she exhaled softly. Home was so far away, not so much geographically but definitely as a possibility; Lionel had made certain that Cassi could never go home as long as he was alive.

A bitter draft danced along her spine and she knew someone had just walked into the yoga studio from outside where the temperatures were hovering in the forties. Why did people always pop in for information when the class was clearly already finished? "Sorry but you missed the class. Schedule's on the door if you want to—"

"Hello, Cassi."

The breath wilted in her lungs, threatening to wheeze out in a painful gasp if she wasn't careful. She turned slowly to face the man whose voice she hadn't heard for years yet remembered with a ferocity that shocked her.

"Nobody calls me that anymore," she said, her gaze sliding over him in a quick but wary appraisal. Time had been good to him. Not that he hadn't started out with an advantage in that department, but his boyish cuteness in high school had hardened into the kind of take-a-girl's-breath-away attractive that often found its way onto the movie screen. Tommy had that quality in spades.

Except Tommy Bristol had always hated the attention his good looks had brought his way and never would've tolerated fame well. Unlike Cassi, who had basked in any light that had shone her way. She blinked away the unexpected tears, unsure where they originated from but felt certain they could gain her no ground with the man assessing her as intently as she had assessed him.

"How'd you find me?" she asked. No one in her current circles knew her true name.

He shrugged, but a hard light entered his eyes that she didn't care for.

"Been a while…" She let the rest of her sentence trail.

"That it has," he agreed easily. "You've been busy."

She cut him a short glance. "A girl has to make a living."

"Not typically on the backs of others," he returned mildly.

Put that way, it sounded so sordid, so mean. She supposed to him it probably looked like that. A minor ache bloomed somewhere in her chest for the dry, dusty remains of whatever had once softened him toward her. Would it change things if he knew how her life had spiraled to the place she was mired in now? Likely not, given the cool chill coming from those ocean-blue eyes so like her own. In school, kids had snickered that they were probably related. She cocked her head and wondered what he saw when he looked at her. A thief? A liar? Perhaps both. But she was certain when he looked at her he didn't see a long-lost friend. Yes, there it was again, that ache, ghosting across her chest, squeezing painfully. Why did it have to be him? Anyone but him.

"Not everything is as it seems," she said, surprising herself at the effort. She shouldn't have wasted her time.

"And most of the time…it is," he countered.

"Not all of it is true," she murmured, glancing away so as not to see the derision in the cruel twist of his lips.

He sighed and the sound pulled her attention. He almost looked…regretful. But it was gone in one laborious heartbeat. "Cassi…you're under arrest. You had to know this was coming sooner or later."

She refused to answer. It was probably rhetorical, anyway. "And you're going to be the one to bring me in, huh?"

"That's right."

Keep thinking that, Tommy boy. He was blocking the front exit. She couldn't count on outrunning him to the back exit. Besides, the latch sometimes stuck and she figured if luck had been on her side, she wouldn't be facing down Thomas Bristol at that moment so she wasn't about to lean on luck for favors. That left one way out. Not the way she preferred, but there wasn't much she could do about that.

"What if I'm innocent?" she asked, testing the waters one last time.

"Then a court of law will decide that. Get your stuff. We have a hard night of driving ahead of us and I want to get moving."

She took in his stance, the way it seemed he might know her next move before she made it, and she knew no matter their history, he wasn't going to be swayed by the pull of old times.

This man was going to arrest her.

TRINITY MOON—AKA CASSANDRA Amelia Nolan—still had the delicate features of a fallen angel, though where laughter and mischief had once lit up her face, shadows now lurked in her eyes. Eyes that had once captivated his soul and made his world spin out of control with wanting something so badly. It was hard to believe he was staring at the woman who had once been his friend, confidante and the secret love of his life until reality intruded and sent them running away from one another.

"Are you going to tell me how you found me or should I guess? As far as I know I didn't leave a trail of bread crumbs," she quipped, interrupting his thoughts.

"Wasn't easy. You're a slippery one," he said. He left out the part where he'd been tracking her movements for about two months. Just as he'd been getting ready to pounce, she'd gotten squirrelly and taken off again. She never used the same name twice but she left a path of troubled and perplexed victims who were lighter in the pocketbook for making her acquaintance. He still had a hard time believing the evidence but it was all there in black-and-white. His childhood friend had become the worst kind of thief—the kind who wormed her way into the warm, trusting bosom of strangers and then split with their hard-earned cash.

It was near unfathomable but plain despicable. And he was going to bring her in.

She must've read it in his eyes for she gestured. "Can I get a quick shower?" she asked. "It'll just take a minute. I promise."

The answer should've been a short and succinct no. It was no worry of his if he hauled her back to West Virginia stinking of sweat but it seemed a small thing she was asking. The room was warm even though the thermostat had been turned off for the night. He knew her routine by now. He knew her license was fake and that she'd likely never been to India in spite of her claims that she'd studied under some swami guru while traveling abroad to find her inner sense of peace. He had to hand it to her, for a girl who grew up with a silver spoon in her mouth, she'd become damn resourceful. In the two weeks since finding her, he'd lurked around the edges of her life, waiting for the right opportunity to bring her down.

There was no malice—he was just doing his job. Therefore, her request for a shower seemed a decent thing to grant. Perhaps in a slight nod to the time when she'd been his only friend in a world that had turned against him, he agreed.

And that was mistake number one.

CASSI SMILED WITH LIPS gone cold and forced humble gratitude into her gaze for his small concession. She didn't recognize the hard man before her even though he wore the face of someone who had once been very dear to her. She knew he wore a gun under his jacket, that he carried a badge of some sort though she didn't know from what agency, and that he was going to haul her in on charges that she was certainly guilty of—if you went by the letter of the law—but could explain with complete sincerity if he'd but give her the chance.

Only, she knew there would be no chances to explain to this man. He was hard as granite and functioning as a robotic arm of the law.

So after she set the water temperature in the shower stall and made small appropriate shower noises, she quickly jerked a sweatshirt over her sweaty sports bra and slipped on her tennis shoes.

She climbed out the bathroom window to the fire escape and melted into the frigid night.

And if she felt a twinge of guilt for duping him, it was eclipsed by the knowledge that she was not cut out for prison life and not even Tommy Bristol was going to make her test that assumption.

THOMAS SWORE SOMETHING ugly when he entered the bathroom and found it empty. She'd given him the slip. Just like that. Smiled and disappeared like smoke on the wind. He should've seen it coming, but he hadn't. Was it necessary to log that in the report? That he'd been momentarily fogged by a sense of nostalgia and inadvertently let a wanted woman slip through his fingers like a rookie cop fresh out of the academy?

Hell, he wasn't even a cop. He was an FBI agent. And he should know better.

The fact was…he did know better. Cassi had always managed to turn the contents of his brain upside down until all the smarts just tumbled to the floor, useless. Apparently, not even the years between them had changed that.

No. He didn't think he'd include this first meeting in the report.

He knew where she was going. He'd just have to beat her there before she split again. Knowing her, she already had another destination in her mind, another identity to assume. She was becoming damn good at disappearing but he was damn good at finding those who didn't want to be found.

That was why her dossier had landed in his lap. At first, he'd been stunned stupid, staring down at the file in his hands, hardly hearing a word his supervisor was saying about the case. He caught bits and pieces, none of it good, and by the time he'd recovered from seeing Cassi staring back at him from a dated driver's license photo, he'd lost most of what had been said and had to follow up on his own so as not to let on that there was a definite conflict of interest for him on this one.

He should've given the file right back with the admission that they'd grown up together and he'd once harbored romantic feelings for her, but his lips sealed shut and the words died, trapped in his mouth. If anyone should bring Cassi in, shouldn't it be him? He'd make sure she was treated with respect and even if he couldn't help, perhaps having a familiar face might lessen the fear of being taken into custody.

Then he read her file and he'd been appalled, no, horrified at how much she'd changed since they saw each other last, more than a handful of years ago. Actually, it'd been their freshman year in separate colleges. She went off to Boston University while he was going to junior college with the hopes of transferring to a state school or university, but Cassi had never found education particularly alluring and never graduated. Instead, she fell into a party crowd that Thomas gave a wide berth. He had no use for overprivileged Yanks with inflated egos and ridiculous credit card limits.

It had never mattered much that they came from different worlds until then. Cassi started to change—or maybe she would've said that he was the one who changed; it didn't really matter at this point—and hot, angry words had been said, mean enough to sever ties and fracture an enduring friendship. He hated to admit it but he'd never stopped nursing that particular wound, no matter how hard he tried.

And now the devious woman had just proven she didn't give a rip for anything they might've shared when they were young. So why the hell was he?

He gave the studio one final sweep just in case she'd doubled back, though he instinctively knew she wouldn't. But he wasn't about to make another rookie mistake. He left because he knew Cassi wasn't going to hang around this town much longer.

And one thing was for sure, he was ending this night with Cassi in custody.

CHAPTER TWO

CASSI VACILLATED BETWEEN plain getting the hell
out of the city with just the clothes on her back or
returning to her tiny apartment to get a few things
first. In the end, she decided—a bit fretfully—that
she couldn't skip town without her date book at the
very least. It seemed a small thing but every little
scrap of information she'd managed to pull together
on Lionel Vissher was in that damn thing and she
wasn't about to let it get tossed in the trash when the
landlord realized she'd bailed.

So, against every screaming bit of intuition in her
head, she returned to her place. But she eschewed
the front walk up and opted for the fire escape instead, just in case someone was watching—and by
someone she meant that cold-eyed stranger trying to
pass himself off as a former friend.

She jimmied the window and slid it open quietly.
She always kept it unlocked for this very purpose.
While most people might worry about their posses-
sions, she didn't own anything she couldn't walk
away from except for her date book and she doubted

anyone looking for easy cash was going to zero in on the beaten-up old date book. It looked as if it'd been chewed up by a rabid dog and then run over by a semi.

Forgoing the light, she made her way to the night-stand beside her bed, intent on getting her book and then racing out of there. She had already purchased a bus ticket for this very occasion, though admittedly, she hadn't thought she was going to be using it quite this soon. She'd come to New York following a lead but it took time to ferret out details of Lionel's life before he met her mom, and she'd only just started to flesh out her new identity so she hadn't made contact yet with her mark.

Just as her hand closed on the worn leather, the light flicked on, momentarily blinding her.

"You really ought to be less sentimental," a voice said, scaring the crap out of her in one breath and causing her to swear softly in the next. "If you'd split town you might've earned yourself another couple of months free and clear, but in the end, it's always the mementos that get people."

She turned. "It's not a memento. It's the key to getting my life back," she said evenly, pissed at her-self for breaking one of her own rules—carrying her valuables with her at all times. She should've kept her date book in her backpack with the rest of her essentials but she'd left it behind this morning when she'd realized her backpack had ripped a seam. She'd planned on buying a new one.

Tommy gestured and pulled out a pair of hand-cuffs. She eyed the stainless steel and lifted her chin. "Aren't you even curious?" she asked.

"No."

She made a face. "What happened to you? You used to have a heart. Being a cop has leached all the humanity out of you."

His expression didn't change, and the fact that he was implacable as stone in spite of their history served to make her wish things had turned out differently between them, but it didn't make her want to turn herself in. If she allowed Tommy to bring her in, Lionel would win and there was no way in hell she was going to let that happen. "So now what?" she asked, stalling for time.

"I take you into custody and we drive to my field office in Pittsburgh, where I will turn you over to the proper authorities."

"Sounds like a walk in the park," she said, then sighed. "Well, I guess it was bound to happen sooner or later."

He eyed her with suspicion. "So you're willing to come quietly this time?" He glanced around the tiny apartment. "No windows you're planning to crawl out of? Or maybe you have a trapdoor somewhere that drops you down to the first floor?"

"Well, there is the trash chute but I don't really like the idea of getting dirty," she quipped. When her answer didn't elicit even the tiniest of grins, she said, "Can you blame me? What would you've done in my situation?"

"I'm not in your situation, nor would I be, so there's no sense in trying out hypothetical scenarios."

Cassi glared. "I liked you better when you were a loner without friends."

A tiny muscle moved in his cheek and she wondered at it. Had she struck a nerve? It seemed cruel to remind him of how they met but he wasn't making this any easier by acting like a robot. Well, what a waste of time anyway. She wasn't sticking around to smooth out the edges of their reunion. Better to get this over with and deal with her hurt feelings later. Like when she was on a bus traveling far enough away to kick him off her trail.

She came forward and put her wrists together in a show of surrender but she had no intentions of going quietly. In one of her identities she worked at a dojo. She and the instructor had a thing and she was a very able student. Suffice to say...she knew a few things that would come in handy right about now.

"Turn around," he instructed and she gave him a sad, wounded look that said she was hurt because he didn't trust her. And if he were smart, he wouldn't. But she had a hunch that he wasn't as hard as he put on. There was a soft spot underneath all that marble and she was going to poke at it to her advantage. He seemed to weigh the options heavily and she almost thought she'd overestimated her ability to persuade him but he finally relented with a gruff admonishment, "If you try anything I will hog-tie you for the entire trip back. You got it?" and she knew she'd won.

She bit her lip but nodded. "Scout's honor."

Good thing she'd never been a Scout. Shame on Tommy. He should've remembered that.

THOMAS CLICKED OPEN the handcuffs and came toward her, his gut reacting adversely to the lump of lead sitting in it. She looked scared, even though she was trying to hide it. She'd always tried to hide her true feelings from everyone, except him.

A part of him was itching to know the details of her messed-up life but he kept that curiosity under lock and key. He didn't need to know. When he looked at her he tried not to see the girl he'd fallen helplessly in love with back when they were kids. He'd been the quiet loner and she'd been the popular girl who attracted people like bees to honey. Gorgeous and wealthy, spoiled and willful, yet for whatever reasons, she'd befriended him during a time when nothing in his young life had seemed right. She might not have realized it but that one act of kindness had sealed her fate. And his, as well. By the time they reached high school, his heart had secretly belonged to her.

She could've had it all. Hell, she practically already had at the age of sixteen. So when had it all gone to shit?

Thomas advanced and as he prepared to click the handcuffs in place—his mind in all sorts of places but not focused as it should've been—he was taken off guard by what she did next.

The woman clocked him.

Painful stars burst behind his eyes and he crashed to the floor, but before he landed he grabbed blindly and by sheer luck managed to snag her sneakered foot, sending her tumbling to the worn carpet, as well. She landed with a soft grunt and tried to kick his hand free but he was already losing the birds flying around his head and he lunged at her. She turned into a kicking, scratching she-devil and it was all he could do to keep from getting her size nine in his face.

"Let me go," she demanded as they struggled, but he'd managed to put his full weight on top of her and the last part came out as an outraged gasp. She was shorter than him but at five foot nine she wasn't a petite little thing. She'd always been curvy in all the right spots and if it hadn't been for the pulsing agony in his temple he might've been distracted by all that soft, womanly flesh pressed tightly against him. When he was a teen he'd fantasized about what it might feel like to be hip to hip with this woman, but in his wildest dreams he never imagined that when it happened she'd be doing her best to kill him.

He managed to secure both her hands but it wasn't easy. The woman had skills. Both of them were breathing hard, which made her breasts push against his chest and he could feel the soft caress of her breath against his face. She smelled of cinnamon candy and some kind of herbal lotion or oil that you might find in a specialty store. It wasn't patchouli— that stuff made him sneeze—but it was something that someone might enjoy as an incense. Whatever it was, the scent called up images of warm bodies sliding against one another in a darkened room, urgent whispers and hands caressing. Hell, did she douse herself in some kind of aphrodisiac? He blinked hard against the images his mind happily threw at him in concert with the aroma assault and he tightened his grip on her hands until she couldn't do much more than twist beneath him. He stared down into a pair of deadly calculating eyes that radiated anger and retribution and he knew if she had half a chance she'd brain him and be on her merry way.

"You're coming with me," he said from between gritted teeth, his breathing labored for more reasons than the physical exertion. He was horrified to admit he was aroused. He could only hope she didn't realize that the bulge pressing against her wasn't only the ridge from his jeans.

Chest heaving as she caught her breath, she gave him a mocking glare as she pointed out one crucial detail. "The minute you let go of my hands I'm going to get free. You have the advantage right now only because you're holding my hands. You can't stay this way forever."

He narrowed his gaze. "Don't make this worse on yourself. You're already in a heap of trouble. The ride is over."

"You don't know anything about what's going on. All you know is what *he's* told everyone."

He shouldn't ask but he did anyway. "He who?"

"Lionel Vissher. My stepfather."

"What's he got to do with the people you've swindled out of thousands of dollars?"

"I haven't swindled anyone," she shot back and he could only stare. The last time he checked, stealing people's identity and then their cash was indeed swindling. But whatever word she used to describe it…it was still illegal. And she was guilty. "I borrowed a little to survive. I plan to pay them back."

"Sure you do."

Her lips tightened and he found it vaguely ironic that she was offended by his disbelief. "I have every name of every person I ever borrowed from and I will pay them back as soon as I get Lionel out of my family's bank account."

"So these past two years you've been running from the law, you've actually been hunting down information on your stepfather?" he asked.

"Yes," she answered, a flare of hope in her voice. "That's exactly it. I never actually hurt anyone, I mean I know I deceived a few people but harmlessly so. When I pay them back everything will be fine. But if you take me in, I'll never get to clear my name and worse, that snake will continue to live in my family's home sucking up the fortune my father helped build." His brow furrowed and she recognized that look from years ago. She continued quickly. "Think about it, Tommy. Would I do the things they say I've done without a good reason? Why would I? I had plenty of money. I didn't need to steal, not until Lionel came into my life. If you knew what he was really like, you'd be arresting him instead of me." Her hands were slowly losing feeling. She wiggled against him and peered up at him with what she hoped was an expression of vulnerability as she pleaded in a small voice. "Please let me go…you're hurting me, Tommy."

He paused and a myriad of emotions crossed his face. She'd forgotten how handsome he was. He'd epitomized the strong silent type when they were growing up. He'd always been a great listener, even when all she did was complain about problems that in the big scheme of things didn't matter at all. If only she'd realized that then. Now it was too late.

His gaze searched her face and she could almost hope that his silence was evidence of his uncertainty, but she should've known that such a possibility was small for a man like Thomas Bristol. He was a stickler for the rules—which had made a career in law enforcement such a no-brainer. His mouth tightened and his gaze hardened as he told her what was going to happen next. "I'm going to let your hands go and you're going to come quietly."

No way in hell. "Try it and see."

"I don't want to hurt you. Just do yourself a favor and don't fight me."

Was that the tiniest plea couched in that harsh tone? She could only wonder. "Let me go and we won't have to fight."

"You know that's not possible."

"I don't know any such thing. You could walk away, pretend you never found me."

"That's not who I am and I'm not about to change so you can continue using people for your own gain. According to your file, you're a thief and a liar and your free ride stops here."

She scowled. "That's an inflammatory statement,

don't you think? And quite possibly slanderous. Watch yourself, Tommy. Perhaps I'll sue."

His mouth twisted. "Oh, really? I'd like to see you try."

"Get off me, you brute. It's not like you're a lightweight. Perhaps not so many doughnuts and a little more roughage in your diet would help drop some of those pounds," she taunted him, enjoying the flare of anger that followed. It was complete crap, of course. He was built like a Greek god and if she were in a different position, she certainly wouldn't complain about his body on top of hers but that wasn't her reality so the lug needed to get the hell off and quick. If insulting him got the job done she was more than willing to do it. "Oh, man, I can't breathe." She twisted a little beneath him. "Seriously, you're hurting me. I promise I won't do anything, just get off. Okay?"

"Promise?" He eyed her with suspicion.

"My hands are going numb and my ribs are cracking," she said in answer, shifting again under his weight.

"You're the one who put us in this position," he reminded her, but oddly, he didn't move. She inhaled the sharp scent of his skin and when images from the past assaulted her, she kicked them away. She'd never slept with him—a blessing, perhaps, though definitely a serious regret—but they had shared one helluva kiss on her seventeenth birthday. Was he remembering that sizzling moment, as well? Doubtful. The fact that she was suddenly reminded of that moment discomfited her.

"Tommy, I mean it," she said, snapping him out of whatever he was thinking. He shifted slowly, watching her closely. Guess he didn't trust her much after she rattled his teeth. She wouldn't, either, if the roles were reversed. She drew a deep breath, wincing as her ribs complained, then as he let her hands go she shook some circulation back into them before scrambling to her feet.

"Cassi," he warned, advancing toward her as she backed away, her thoughts moving quickly to the best possible escape plan. "There's nowhere for you to go. Think this through. You won't get far."

He underestimated her need to escape. She shrugged, appearing flippant but in truth she was stalling, waiting for the strength to return to her limbs. She was starting to think that's why he stayed on top of her, to weaken her. Well, if it was, it'd worked and it also destroyed her hope that he'd stayed put simply because he liked being there. Ouch. There's a blow to the ol' ego. She flexed her fingers and gave him a hard look of her own. "Sorry, Tommy. I can't. There's no way I can make you understand and that's a tragedy but I'm not going anywhere with you. That man killed my mother and I'm going to prove it somehow. It's the only chance I have of making things right, so if you want to take me in you'll have to kill me first."

CHAPTER THREE

SHE MOVED QUICKLY BUT Thomas had anticipated her move and dodged with her. Just as his fingers grabbed for her arm, she spun out of his reach. She was making her way to the door. He knew if she made it past that threshold she'd disappear and it would take months to track her down again. That wasn't going to happen. He didn't have time to zap her with a Taser, and he sure as hell wasn't going to shoot her—though another agent might've, seeing as she'd already committed an assault against an officer—so he went old school.

This time when he tackled her to the ground, he didn't waste time trying to subdue her. She kicked and bucked but he reared back and cut a clean right hook across her jaw.

She stilled and went limp beneath him. Thomas exhaled loudly, wishing to hell he hadn't had to do that, but he figured it was the lesser of two evils at that moment.

"Damn it, Cassi," he muttered sharply, feeling like shit. It went against his personal beliefs—men who hit women were scum—but she'd given him no choice. Still, even knowing this, it didn't lessen the feeling he'd just crossed a line. A good agent didn't let the past affect his actions. If he'd hesitated, she would've gotten away and he would have had to explain why to his superiors.

Pulling his handcuffs, he made short work of securing her. He climbed to his feet and took a quick look around the cramped apartment. *Ugly* was the appropriate word for it, he thought as he made a short circuit. Peeling yellowed wallpaper covered the walls, and brown, matted carpet covered the floor. He doubted anything in this place belonged to Cassi. From what he remembered, thrift store garbage wasn't exactly her decorating style, which told him she'd rented the apartment furnished. There was nothing personal in this space, nothing that would suggest she actually lived there. She had the essentials but nothing else. The occupant of this house lived a transient existence. Here today, gone tomorrow, which fit Cassi's M.O. Still, he opened a few drawers and rifled through the contents. A grim part of him was hoping to find evidence of drugs because maybe he could understand why she'd turned so bad if he found she suffered an addiction. But when his search came up empty, he couldn't say he wasn't relieved, too.

No pictures, no personal effects. What a lonely

life, he reflected for a minute before returning to where Cassi lay unconscious. He'd lied. He'd wanted to know her story, her reasons, but he'd be damned if he let himself slide down that slippery slope. He didn't cause her to make her bad choices. He had to keep sight of that before he went and did something foolish, like trust her to tell him the truth and then fall hook, line and sinker for her lies.

Thomas hoisted her onto his shoulder, grunting under the weight and taking care not to notice the plump, round curves of her ass right at his face. There were a million different reasons why he shouldn't be attracted to her, but his hand itched to touch her and it only served to sour his mood further.

Why Cassi? Of all the women in the world…why her? There were too many memories, too many unresolved feelings, just flat out, too much of everything. He'd been a fool to take this case but what was done was done. He'd see it through, no matter what. And he absolutely *would not* give in to the strange and inappropriate urge to give that firm ass a nice squeeze.

He passed a neighbor or two but didn't stop to explain why he was carting away an unconscious woman on his shoulder, nor did he flash his badge. Funny, no one asked any questions. That said a lot about the neighborhood she was living in. Definitely a far cry from the digs she was accustomed to, that was for sure.

Cassi had lived in the rich part of town where they grew up in Bridgeport, West Virginia. Her house had been the most lavish, ridiculous piece of masonry Thomas had ever seen. Cassi came from old money and she'd enjoyed all that it had afforded from top-shelf education to high-society circles. Hell, she'd even had a coming-out party when she'd turned sixteen just like they did in the Old South. His upbringing hadn't been so privileged. Until he'd been put in Mama Jo's care, his home life had been hell. He didn't like to spend much time remembering those days. And there was no reason for him to, either, but a memory floated unbidden from his past. Odd, given the circumstances, but it flashed real and tangible before he could stop it.

"You like her," a young Christian had said, his voice wise for a twelve-year-old kid who still slept with a ratty teddy bear that smelled so bad it probably scared away vermin. Owen glanced up from whittling on his ash twig, interest in his eyes at their brother's sudden proclamation. "So why don't you just ask her out or something?"

Thomas's face had colored. "I don't like her," he protested. "We're just friends. Nothing wrong with that."

They were down by Flaherty's Creek behind

Mama Jo's house "stayin' out of mischief" as per Mama's instruction.

"It's s'okay, you know," Christian said, skipping a rock across the water, listening as it splashed to the other side. "If you like her, I mean. She's pretty."

Thomas followed Christian's lead and threw his own rock, giving a short, victorious smile as it skipped one more time than Christian's rock. Finally, he shrugged. "It's not like that," he said. "She's not like most girls. She's—" he scratched at his head "—I don't know, special. She doesn't notice that my clothes aren't brand-spanking-new or that I don't have a bunch of money like the rest of those dumb Yanks do. She thinks I'm funny, too."

"Funny-looking, you mean," quipped Owen with a smothered grin before returning to his whittling.

"Ha-ha. Go back to your stick or I'll tell Poppy Jones a thing or two about you."

Owen narrowed his stare at Thomas, his green eyes darkening. "You wouldn't dare."

"I would." Thomas gave his brother his best shit-eatin' grin. "Like how you stare at the back of her head during class with this dopey look on your face."

Christian cackled and slapped his knee. "You guys both got it bad. You won't see me drooling over some girl. You gotta get them on the hook before you reel them in. And whatever you do, don't let them get their claws into you. If you do, you're done for."

Both Thomas and Owen shared sour looks but they couldn't exactly say anything to the contrary, because even as the youngest, Christian had the girls going nuts over him. In fact, they trailed after the kid like he was made of chocolate and they all wanted to take a bite, but Christian never let anyone catch him…at least not for long.

Owen straightened and examined his work. A rudimentary, but not half-bad-looking bear totem stared back at him. He tucked the finished work into his back pocket and went to stand by Thomas. "You know, you're right. Cassi is different than other girls. She's cool and I hope you two stay friends a long time. I mean it."

That quiet statement resonated with Thomas, striking a chord deep inside him. "Thanks, man. Me, too. Yeah…I mean…" He shifted on the balls of his feet and admitted something private. "It would be cool if we did but she's got all those rich friends…I don't know. I don't really fit in with her world."

Owen knew a thing or two about not fitting in, but he shrugged and said, "Who cares what her rich friends think? Cassi wants you in her world so forget about them. She's the one who matters, right?"

"Yeah, I guess," he agreed.

"So make the most of it then. And don't let her go."

Thomas shoulder-bumped him with a grin. "Look at you all wise and stuff." They shared a laugh and then Thomas sobered. "Thanks."

Owen grinned in answer and opened his mouth to say something but he never got the chance. Christian barreled into them both with a loud battle cry and they all went tumbling into the creek for one last cutthroat game of Drown the Rat before the sun set on the horizon.

The recollection of their laughter drew a soft smile from his lips. He didn't know why that memory, of all the ones tucked away in his mind, rose to the surface but at least it elicited warmth instead of pain, like the ones before he came to live with Mama Jo.

As far as he was concerned, his life before age twelve didn't exist. Shaking off the odd melancholy, he grabbed his cell phone and stopped short of giving his superior a status update. He figured there was no rush. The prisoner was secured and it was a five-hour drive back to headquarters. With nothing but time to pass, he thought he'd use the opportunity to satisfy the questions in his head.

It was a foolish idea. Somewhere in his mind there was a stern voice of reason warning him that this was a bad plan but he wasn't listening at the moment. He could charter a plane on the Bureau's dime and be there in half the time but he wanted to drive—and he wanted to spend time with her.

CASSI CAME TO WITH A GROAN that was immediately followed by a muttered curse under her breath when she realized she was handcuffed.

Her jaw hurt like hell. He'd punched her. She hadn't seen that coming. Tommy wasn't the kind of man who hit women. At least he hadn't been. But her jaw ached like a son of a bitch so there was no denying what had happened.

She opened her eyes slowly and spared Tommy a short accusatory glance. "I can't believe you hit me."

"You were uncooperative."

"Is it your habit now to hit women?" Given his childhood—she was one of a very small group who knew the details—it was a nasty question. His jaw tightened but she refused to feel bad. He'd punched her in the face. That wasn't something she was going to forget anytime soon. There was also the fact that she was handcuffed like a common criminal to deal with, too. "I'd have thought that was one thing you'd never do. Seems I'm not the only who's changed over the years."

"I didn't want to. You left me no choice," he said.

"You had a choice. You could've let me go." His

silence told her how futile that argument was but she was more than angry with the man—her feelings were bruised that he'd purposefully hurt her. The Tommy in her memory would've beaten anyone to a pulp if they'd laid a hand on her. Now he was the one dealing out the punches. Her eyes stung. She wouldn't cry in front of him. Instead she allowed a small smirk even though the action cost her as a sharp pain followed. She gingerly worked her jaw. The petty victory could only buoy her spirits for a brief moment but it was enough to keep the tears from surfacing. "You didn't by any chance happen to grab a small, black leather date book on your way out, did you?"

"You aren't going to need a date book where you're going," he answered and she scowled. "No, I didn't grab anything but you from that hovel you called an apartment."

"It wasn't that bad," she shot back, an odd pang of embarrassment for her living conditions getting the better of her. What did she care what he thought? "I've lived in worse."

He glanced at her. "Worse? That's a scary thought. I think I saw a cockroach big enough to cart away a small child."

"That was Charlie. I feed him scraps. I was train- ing him to be an attack roach. A few more veggie burgers and he'd have been better than a guard dog.

I could've sicced him on you," she said dully, feeling ill at the loss of her date book. In her mind, she replayed the scenario again and again, sickened that she'd been so careless with the one important item in her possession.

"So, what's in this date book that's so important?"

She swallowed the burn at the back of her throat. Two years of hard work…gone. Why hadn't she hit him harder? Truth was, she'd pulled her punch a little. She hadn't wanted to hurt him. Not really. Now…hell, she should've knocked his teeth out of his head. She worked her jaw but refused to wince even though the pain felt rooted in her bones. "I guess it doesn't matter, does it?" she said, looking away so he didn't read the despair in her eyes.

"No, I guess it doesn't," he returned, his gaze never leaving the road, the unfeeling bastard. But then, he cut her a quick glance, saying, "But just out of curiosity—"

She closed her eyes. "Just shut up, will you? Whatever's in that date book is none of your damn business, so drop it."

"Fine."

She leaned against the headrest and struggled not to just let it all out and cry her fool head off. At one time she would've bet her life that Tommy would always have her back. The man was integrity personified. Yet, here she was feeling betrayed by the very same man. Cassi twisted so that she could look out the window instead of at the man who was destroying any chance of getting her life back and— ironically—finding justice for her mother.

WHY DID HE FEEL AS IF HE was the one doing something wrong here? Thomas tightened his hands on the steering wheel and wondered if he hadn't made a mistake in driving. Suddenly, that five-hour ride didn't seem like a good idea. And what had he expected? It was unlikely Cassi was going to ignore the handcuffs and chatter away like old times. He wasn't an idiot, even though his actions might indicate otherwise. He'd known all this…but he couldn't resist the possibility of seeing her again…maybe even helping her through this mess she'd made for herself.

And now he felt like an idiot for even entertaining such thoughts. She wasn't a damsel in distress. The woman was a far cry from the girl he'd known so long ago. This woman was a criminal…with a nasty punch. His head was still ringing.

So knowing all this…why was he feeling bad for her? He cast a quick glance her way then looked away again. Was that remorse in her expression? Her face, tilted away from him was in profile as she leaned against the glass. A tendril of something long lost kindled to life and reminded him of how he'd thought he was in love with her once.

"Tell me what you think it feels like to be in love," a thirteen-year-old Cassi whispered from his memory of a day in late May. She'd been wearing a white sundress that dusted her knees and they'd stolen away to a meadow behind Mama Jo's house on one of the occasions Cassi and her mother had had an argument. During those times, Cassi had often found her way to Thomas's house, even though their homes weren't exactly close. The warm breeze had lifted the honey-hued hair away from her face while her blue eyes had sparked with genuine curiosity. They'd tumbled to the tall grass and lay side by side on their stomachs, watching through the swaying green stalks as squirrels chased each other through the white ash trees and birds dipped and wheeled in the flawless cerulean sky.

He'd known the answer because he felt it every time he looked at her. "I think it makes your stomach all tight like someone's squeezing it real hard, so much so that it hurts, but you don't mind because it makes you want to be around that person, even when you're not really doing anything special."

She wrinkled her nose, not at all pleased with his theory. "That sounds like the stomach flu. Why would anyone want to fall in love if it made them want to throw up? No, I don't think that's how it is at all," she announced firmly. "I think that when you're in love you feel a tickle in your heart and you want to kiss that person all the time."

Thomas's young heart had stuttered at the thought of kissing Cassi. Cassi hadn't noticed though and had simply sighed dreamily, saying, "I can't wait to fall in love. I think I would like to kiss someone who wants to kiss me back." Then an alarming thought had come to her and she sat a little straighter, turning to Thomas. "What if I never find someone who loves me? What if I go my entire life and no one wants to kiss me like that? Oh, Tommy, that's an awful thought. I would die."

And he'd wanted to reassure her that that would never happen because at that very moment he wanted to kiss her so bad his brain had simply stopped functioning. Then as he thought to lean forward to press his lips against hers in what would've been their first kiss, she'd leaned over and whispered conspiratorially, "Can you keep a secret?" He'd been dumbfounded as she giggled, admitting, "I think I'm going to fall in love with Billy Barton and I'm going to kiss him."

His world had plummeted.

And Cassi's first kiss had been with a boy who could burp the alphabet…not with Thomas. Their kiss wouldn't happen for another four years.

Jerked back to the moment, he suffered the pang

of that bittersweet childhood memory and was happy to push it away and focus on the here and now, not the been and gone.

"You hungry?" he asked gruffly.

She didn't bother to answer.

He withheld a sigh. "Fine. Just asking."

"Why you?" she asked him abruptly. He gave her a quick look and saw the glitter in her eyes. "Isn't there some kind of conflict of interest, seeing as we have a history?" He could've lied but he couldn't bring himself to utter a word. His silence was telling. She barked a short laugh. "You didn't offer that information. Interesting," she said, returning her gaze to the darkened landscape outside the window. "So, it seems Thomas Bristol isn't always Dudley Do-Right when it suits his purposes to bend the rules." She shrugged. "I'm the last person to judge for what you may consider obvious reasons but if there's one thing I never pegged you for, it's a hypocrite."

"I'm not a hypocrite," he bit out, his hackles rising at the mockery.

"Oh? I didn't manage to finish college but I'm pretty sure I have a full grasp of the word's meaning. Please explain to me how you are not indeed a hypocrite, judging by your actions? Is it not required for you to disclose any personal history or relationship with a suspect or prisoner?" He didn't answer, which was good because she continued. "Ah, well. Like

I said, if you're Thomas Bristol, rules are simply guidelines but for everyone else, the law is black-and-white."

It wasn't like that but when she put it that way it sounded pretty damn bad. "You're right. I didn't tell my superior. I wanted—" *to see you again* "—to make sure that you were treated as fairly as possible given the situation. You know if you'd pulled that stunt back there with anyone else you might've gotten yourself killed. Did you think about that at all when you were going all kung fu on my ass?" She refused to look at him. He swore under his breath, wondering why he was wasting his time. "Forget it. You know, you're right. I should've walked away the first time your file crossed my desk. I should've done an about-face and left you to whoever had the misfortune to get your case, but I didn't because at first I thought there had to be a mistake. There's no way the girl I used to know had turned into a criminal. But when I couldn't deny it any longer I wanted to make sure that at the very least, you had someone who would treat you kindly."

At that she gave him a brief look, derision twisting her mouth. "Kindly? This is your version of 'kind'? Pardon me if I don't subscribe to your brand of kindness," she retorted and rubbed gingerly at her jaw with her bound hands.

"You seem to forget you cleaned my clock the first go-round."

The corner of her lips twitched. "Of course I haven't forgotten. I'm just wishing I hadn't pulled my punch. Maybe the situation might have played out differently."

She'd pulled her punch? He nearly did a double take. It'd felt as if she'd beaned him with a hammer. Gone was the girl who'd shied away from anything physical for fear of breaking a nail. "Where'd you learn to be such a bruiser?" he asked.

She didn't look inclined to answer but after a drawn-out pause, she answered coolly. "You'd be surprised what I know."

"At this point no, I wouldn't," he muttered.

CHAPTER FOUR

"I HAVE TO PEE," SHE announced, looking to him to see if he cared. To be honest, she didn't really need to go but it was a plausible excuse to get him to stop the car. They'd been traveling for about an hour and a half, and each mile away from New York and her precious date book made her panic level climb but she kept it under control. It wouldn't do to have him know just how desperate she was feeling about this whole situation. She didn't need to give him yet another piece of leverage to use against her. So, the excuse of bodily function seemed the best bet.

"How bad?" he asked.

"I'm about to soak your leather interior. Is that bad enough?"

"Can you hold it another few minutes? I think there's an off-ramp coming up. Might as well gas up while we're at it. If we're lucky there might be a McDonald's or something."

"Yum. Mystery meat. I'm a vegan, by the way," she sniffed.

"Since when?"

"Since now," she snapped. It wasn't true. Trinity Moon had been a vegan but Cassi Nolan loved meat. Still, she didn't like him thinking that he knew her that well and she was willing to continue the farce if it threw Tommy off. "I don't eat anything with a face."

"Well, I'm pretty sure they remove the face before they throw the animal on the grill," he said, eliciting a scowl on her part.

"Now you're just being crude. Typical."

"Listen, you can order a salad. How's that?"

She'd really rather sink her teeth into a cheeseburger but she nodded stiffly. It burned like acid but she offered a terse thank-you. Best to make it look genuine. They were somewhere outside Philadelphia and she had no cash on her. That posed a significant problem. If she didn't have any cash, she couldn't pay for a bus ride back to New York, which meant she'd have to hitchhike. The fact that the idea of thumbing a ride with a stranger didn't scare her as much as it should was a sign that she was, indeed, desperate to get back to the city. Hitchhiking, under normal circumstances, was just plain stupid.

An alternate thought came to her. She slid her gaze over to Tommy and took in the details of the car. It was your basic government-issue sedan, which also meant it was an automatic. Score one for her, since she'd never learned how to drive a manual.

When they pulled over, he'd gas up, which would take care of that issue and she could make it back to the city and dump the car before they could catch her on GPS. She bit back the smile but allowed herself the first real breath since being captured. She had a plan.

THOMAS TOOK THE FIRST off-ramp that indicated there was food and gas, but before he parked the car, he made a slow sweep of the area.

"What are you doing?" she asked, squirming a little in her seat. "Remember me? The woman with an immediate and personal issue? I have to go."

"Just getting my bearings," he said, finally selecting a spot right under a bright streetlamp. He offered her a short smile. "This isn't my first apprehension. History or not, I'm not taking any chances."

There was something of a dark expression that flitted across her face and he almost got back on the freeway. She was up to something. It'd been a while but he recognized the cunning look in her eyes that she was doing her best to blanket. He turned and tried to level with her. "Listen, I know you're probably thinking of a dozen different ways to get away from me but don't waste your time. I've done this more times than you know. I don't want to hurt you but I will disable you if need be in order to get the job done. You got it?"

She had no reason to doubt his words. She could see that Tommy wasn't the same person but she had to believe that deep down he still felt something for her, even if it was buried and nearly suffocated beneath the layers of time. Still, she wasn't willing to bet her life on it so she had to think of Tommy as nothing more than an obstacle. It should be easy, seeing as she could feel the bruise forming under her skin from his knuckles. Her gaze hardened but her mouth trembled as she said, *"I have to pee."*

"All right, all right. I heard you. Just making sure we're on the same page before you go and do something stupid. I've seen that look on your face. It's the one that signals trouble."

"You don't know me any longer. You shouldn't presume to know any look of mine, Tommy. Trouble or otherwise," she retorted. "Now can we stop with the chatter and get on with the need at hand?" She lifted her bound wrists and he laughed. She actually thought he was going to take off those manacles? She frowned at his soft chuckle. "What's so funny? Surely you don't expect me to manage the bathroom without the use of my hands."

"I'm sure you'll manage. Get creative," he said, getting out of the car. He had a feeling Cassi could manage just about anything she put her mind to in her present occupation. According to her file, she was a chameleon. She melted into her surroundings and took on a persona flawlessly. One thing that bothered him the minute he picked up her file was something that he had no business wanting to know but he did anyway…why did she stick to the East Coast? She would've stood a better chance at evasion if she'd skipped to the West, but she'd stayed within a certain area, almost as if she were following a pattern. Didn't make sense for someone who was just looking to rip people off. That's the part that bothered him. Or maybe he was just loath to believe that the girl of his memory had truly turned out bad.

He walked her to the restroom and she gave him a scowl for not accommodating her desire to free her hands but he didn't trust her. Besides, he wouldn't trust anyone in this position. She was in his custody, not a date.

"I'll be waiting," he said.

"Fabulous," she muttered and kicked the door shut. He had no doubt she was imagining that it'd been his head.

CASSI PACED THE GRIMY FLOOR of the rest stop bathroom, her bottom lip scraping against her teeth as she wondered how to get out of this situation. She found it vaguely disturbing that Tommy had seen right through her. She'd have to be more careful— that is if she couldn't manage to ditch him. There was a sharp knock at the door and his muffled voice told her to hurry up.

She narrowed her stare at the warped and ugly door then dropped her gaze to the floor, looking for something to pick the lock on the cuffs. She found a broken pen in the corner, nearly covered by a sopping paper towel. She tried not to think too hard about where that pen had been in a previous life. By the looks of the floor, it was nowhere pretty. She broke off the metal clip and worked it into the small hole for the cuff key.

Another sharp rap caused sweat to bead her forehead even though it was freezing in the cramped bathroom. "Gimme a minute," she yelled. "A little privacy please!"

He grumbled something on the other side but didn't try to come in. She thanked her stars for the smallest blessings and worked harder at freeing the lock. She'd practiced this before using a bobby pin but this was a bit trickier. Just as she was about to give up, the lock sprang and the cuffs slid open. She exhaled softly. She had to make it look as if she hadn't messed with them so she clicked the manacles back on loosely, checking to make sure she could easily slide out of them. She risked a tremulous smile for her accomplishment but smothered it before walking out of the bathroom.

Tommy's nose had reddened from the cold. He

gave her a once-over and she held her breath as his gaze fastened briefly on her cuffs. When she lifted her chin and met his stare head-on he seemed satisfied that everything was as it should be. He took hold of her arm and walked her back to the car.

"Such a gentleman," she quipped as he opened the door for her.

"Do you ever give that acid tongue of yours a rest? I see time hasn't done much for your disposition."

She glared. "Excuse me for not being a chipper little companion for your road trip."

"Cassi, I'm just doing my job. Would you really rather have had someone else hauling your butt back? Because that can be arranged. All I have to do is make a call and someone else can be here and I can guarantee you they won't give a rat's ass if you have to pee or if you're hungry. I'm just trying to make this as painless as possible but if you're not interested in the kindness I'm showing you...just say the word."

She swallowed and blinked back a sudden wash of tears. For a moment he was the Tommy she remembered. He'd always had a way of grounding her when she went a little crazy. He was that solid, calming influence that had kept her from losing herself in the ridiculous circles she often traveled. And what he was saying right now...well, she could see the logic of it. She supposed she was glad it was Tommy. Especially since someone else likely would've double-checked her cuffs after she exited the bathroom.

A twinge of regret filtered through her. But if he knew the whole story, she could almost bet that he'd understand.

The only problem? He wasn't willing to listen to her side of the story. So was it really her fault that she was about to do what she had to do?

A part of her wished she could just sit down and show him the evidence she'd collected so far. He might even have valuable insights, maybe even dig out some leads she might've missed. A small ache spread across her chest and a pinprick of nostalgia, sharp and deadly, pierced her mind, dredging up memories that almost made her cry. She risked a look at Tommy, wondering if she should take the chance and tell him what she knew. But even as she searched his face for a clue as to which way to go, she knew she couldn't tell him. He was an agent. His world was black-and-white. That was the world he knew and understood. And she'd be a fool to try to drag him into the chaotic mess that had become her life.

Once she took her seat, he said, "I'm going to go pay for the gas. Don't touch anything."

"I'll try to restrain myself," she said, but adrenaline had already started to flow through her veins.

He'd taken the keys but there was another skill she'd picked up on her travels…

Keys were unnecessary.

THOMAS PUSHED OPEN THE scratched and dull glass door of the convenience store and it took him a full second to realize what he was seeing—or more specifically—not seeing.

His car.

And his prisoner.

Somehow, cuffed and without keys, she'd stolen his car.

He muttered a stream of swear words that would've earned him a bar of soap back in the day and shoved the packaged salad and three different choices of dressing he'd purchased for her into the trash.

If it were possible, he could almost see the steam rising from his ears into the chill air. In glaring detail he knew where he'd screwed up. He hadn't checked her cuffs after she'd emerged from the bathroom. Somehow she'd gotten them loose. He'd made sure they were tight when he put them on, which meant she'd sprung the lock when she was out of sight and banked on the fact that he would be distracted by her in general. And she'd banked right.

The weight of his keys resting in his pocket told him that she'd hot-wired the car. Shit. His cell phone was in the car but he had his wallet, badge and gun. He had two choices: Call it in and have an APB put out on her but risk the ridicule of every one of his peers as well as the ire of his superior. Or he could just go after her.

Like there was a choice.

He spied a pay phone and strode to it. He lifted the receiver, swiped his ATM card and punched in his cell number. He doubted she'd answer but if she did, he had an earful for the runaway, former society girl. The phone rang four times before transferring to his voice mail. He hung up and stared at the road where she'd disappeared. Whatever tender nostalgic feelings he'd had for her withered and died.

This time when he caught her—he'd show no mercy.

CHAPTER FIVE

CASSI KNEW SHE DIDN'T HAVE much of a head start on Tommy, maybe an hour at best, as he probably wasted little time in finding a rental car to chase after her. She also couldn't afford to get pulled over driving a government vehicle so while it grated on her nerves to drive so slowly, she kept her speed at the limit and obeyed all traffic rules.

Tommy's cell phone buzzed to life at her hip in the console but she ignored it. No good would come from answering that phone, even if she were tempted to apologize for putting him in a bad spot. She bit her lip and wondered if this was something he could get fired for. He was probably a very good agent. He'd always held such a rigid concept of morality that she'd half wondered how he was ever going to survive high school—particularly theirs—but those smoking good looks of his hadn't hurt and he'd done just fine, even if he never paid much attention to the politics of his peers.

Unlike her. She settled into the seat and set the cruise control. She'd been such an idiot. All the things she'd thought were important had turned out to be as insubstantial as shadows on the wall. No one really cared that she'd been voted Biggest Flirt their senior year or that she'd been named Prom Queen over Tiffani Jenkins in what had been the biggest coup de grâce Winston High School had ever seen. If only high school cred had extended to something that really mattered, such as getting someone to listen to you when you told them your stepfather had killed your mother but made it look like an accident so no one believed you.

She hadn't realized how much she'd taken her family's money and connections for granted until it'd all been yanked away. Two years was a lifetime to wander in exile.

Some days she couldn't quite believe the life she was living.

But if she could put together the scattered puzzle pieces of Lionel Vissher then the whole picture of deception would become clear. At least that's what she hoped would happen.

Her biggest fear, though, was that, even if she managed to prove that Lionel wasn't who he said he was, no one would care and nothing would change. Lionel would continue blowing through her family's fortune and she'd end up in prison.

A chill puckered her skin and she rubbed at

her forearm. Just thinking it made her sick to her stomach.

She may have been born a spoiled princess but she'd become a soldier and she wasn't about to let Lionel win this war.

"Sorry, Tommy," she whispered and then pushed the thought of her childhood friend far away. She didn't have the luxury of nostalgia.

THOMAS HURTLED DOWN the freeway, back to the city, his mind working quickly to assess the situation. He had to regroup, get his head on straight and apprehend the target. It was likely she was returning to her apartment to get whatever she'd left behind— probably the date book she'd asked about—and then she'd take off again. He wasn't going to waste time going back to her apartment. By the time he reached the city, she'd have cleaned out her essentials and moved on, and he could expect to find his vehicle dumped somewhere. He'd already called in the theft, leaving out the part that it was his target who had stolen it. She would need transportation. The closest bus station to her apartment or her place of employment was the best bet as she'd need someplace quick and easily accessible if things got hot.

He grabbed the disposable phone he'd purchased and quickly dialed someone he trusted. Owen, his foster brother and someone he knew would keep things between them, picked up the line.

"Who is this?" Owen asked. It was nearing midnight in California but Owen was still awake, no doubt crunching numbers on some project or deal for his logging company.

"It's me. I need a favor."

"Tommy? What number are you calling from? You okay? You sound funny."

"I'm fine but I have a bit of a situation I'm dealing with and lost my phone. I'm on one of those disposable things."

"Like the ones drug dealers and pimps use so it can't be traced back to them? Must be one helluva situation you're in. So what's the favor?" Owen asked, getting straight to the point. "I'll help if I can."

"You near a computer?"

"Yeah."

"I need you to text me the addresses of the bus stations nearest to Gorkey and Landon Streets in New York City."

"Going on a trip?"

"Not recreationally."

"You sure you're okay?"

"Everything's fine." Or at least it would be once he caught that little escape artist who had managed to make him look like a rookie and a dumb ass with one shot. "I'd do it myself but this disposable isn't internet capable and I don't have time to locate a computer."

"This sounds personal," Owen murmured, and Tommy didn't waste time denying it even if it wasn't exactly true. But Owen didn't press for details, either, which was another reason Tommy picked him instead of Christian, who lived in Manhattan and was always interested in getting the dirt. "All right. Sent. Anything else?"

"No," he answered, a short satisfied smile following as the cell dinged with an arriving text message. "That'll do it. Thanks, man. I'll explain later."

"Can't wait," Owen returned dryly but then added, "Be safe."

"Always."

The line went dead and Thomas tossed the cell on the seat beside him. Both his brothers were solid guys in different ways. They didn't share a drop of blood but Tommy knew Owen and Christian would have his back just as he would always have theirs. That's how Mama Jo had raised them. He missed spending time with them, but the past few months had been consumed with tracking down Cassi, leaving little time to socialize and catch up. Besides, he wasn't the only one whose personal life was submarined by the job. Christian was a bartender at some swanky place, pulling down more money a year than he was, while Owen had his hands full over in the wilds of the Santa Cruz Mountains in California trying to keep his logging company alive in an economy that had determined logging was something of a dirty word.

They'd scattered but it was rare that they didn't connect a few times a month. And he was feeling the separation. He made a mental promise to pop in and at least say hello to Mama Jo after he dragged Cassi back to West Virginia.

He missed Mama Jo's cooking.

And right about now he was thinking he needed one of her signature finger thumps on the back of his skull for being such a class-A idiot.

CASSI DUMPED THE CAR IN A relatively safe place so it wouldn't get stripped overnight and then hopped a cab back to her apartment. She didn't stroll through the front door but used the fire escape like before, only this time she did a thorough search of the place before she let her guard down. When she was certain Tommy wasn't hiding behind a shower curtain or closet door, she gathered her essentials, including the stuffed date book and the prepaid bus ticket to Jersey and then with one last look around the small place she'd called home for such a brief time, she disappeared out the window.

With the familiar weight of her backpack against

her shoulder blades and the ticket in her hand, her thoughts returned to her situation. She hadn't exactly finished her business in New York when Tommy busted in on her but with the authorities closing in, she didn't have a choice but to lie low for a while. She figured Jersey was a good pick since she could disappear fairly easily into Newark, due to its size. She tended to steer clear of small towns as anonymity was something she prized, and it was damn near impossible to get when everyone wanted to know your business.

She checked the time for the next bus. She had about a half hour to kill. Lucky. It could've been worse. Her stomach growled. Repositioning her pack, she went to the vending machine to check out what kind of toxic waste cleverly packaged as food was available. Hmm, the choices were slim. She settled for a candy bar, figuring the sugar kick might bolster her flagging energy if not help keep her focused.

For some reason she couldn't shake the sense of guilt that shadowed her every movement. Damn Tommy. Why'd he have to be the one to come after her? If it'd been anyone else she could've left without a second glance or even a smidge of concern weighing her down.

She huffed a short breath and took a bite of the candy.

THOMAS SPOTTED HER STANDING in the bus station foyer, chewing slowly, her brow furrowing ever so slightly as if she were wrestling with something. She crumpled the wrapper and threw it in the trash can with a little more force than was required and the expression of consternation was replaced with resolve.

Whatever had her bothered was gone. Thomas pulled his cuffs. Time to make his move.

He moved quietly but with purpose, his eye on the target. He kept to her peripheral vision but bad luck must've been riding on his shoulder for she turned and they locked eyes. Panic registered in hers and she bolted.

Her long legs ate up the dirty tile, putting more distance between them, pushing past the other people waiting for the incoming charter. Desperation gave her the edge. His heart hammered with the exertion but he wasn't about to give up. He'd chase her off a cliff if need be, but she wasn't getting away this time.

"Freeze," he bellowed, causing a number of people to stop and stare, but she kept going. He didn't think it would work but it'd been worth a try. He put all his energy into narrowing the gap between them and he closed in on her. She was nearly within his grasp but she dodged just as he made a grab for her. If he could've managed it, he would've shouted a few choice curse words but, as it was, his lungs were burning, screaming from the stale station air.

She burst outside and darted left to slip past a slightly open gate that led to the maintenance yard and slammed it shut, locking it behind her seconds before he could get to it. He slammed into the gate hard and shook it with both fists when he realized she was beyond his reach.

"Cassi, don't," he warned, his chest heaving as his fingers curled around the cold, rough-textured metal. She stopped and turned. Her breath curled in a teasing cloud before evaporating into the night. She held his stare and he could almost sense her hesitation even though she seemed poised to run. He grabbed on to that hope, distant and fleeting as it may be. "I don't want you to get hurt. If you keep running, it'll only get worse. You'll become hunted by every single law enforcement agency in the United States. There will be nowhere to hide and if you continue to run…they will use lethal force to bring you down."

"I'm not a criminal," she whispered. "I'm just trying to get to the truth."

"What truth?"

"I told you."

He ignored that. Everyone had a story or a reason for doing what they did but it didn't lessen the crime. "What about the people you took advantage of? The people who took you in and bought whatever fairy tale you put together so that you could drain their savings and split town?"

She sucked in a breath. "I never drained anyone's savings. Who told you that?"

The fact that she sounded outraged and hurt he found baffling. "Do you even know the charges leveled against you?" he asked.

"No, but I can't believe they're serious enough to sic the FBI on me."

He ticked off the charges. "Grand theft, fraud, identity theft...fiduciary elder abuse... Cassi, these are pretty hefty charges. You won't be able to run forever. You will be caught."

"What are you talking about? I never did any of those things. I admit, I borrowed some money from a few people but nothing that would be missed or would devastate their finances. And I told you that I planned to pay them back."

"Borrow?"

"Yes."

"Borrowing implies consent and your victims weren't given the choice. You took without asking."

"I will pay them back," she maintained stubbornly.

"It doesn't matter. There's a warrant for your

arrest. You're going to be brought to justice sooner or later. Make it easy on yourself and stop running."

"So you believe I did these things?" she asked, her stance rigid, her stare boring into his, almost daring him to answer. "Grand theft? Elder abuse? Do you really think I could do these things? Me?"

He shook his head, his heart heavy in his chest. "It's not about what I think you're capable of...it's what you've done. I have to bring you in."

"What if you're wrong? What if all those charges were false? What if someone was trying to keep me out of the picture and painting me as a criminal was the best way to get rid of me? What if the real criminal was the one giving you the bad information?"

"What about Barbara Hanks? Winifred Jones? Or Isaac Wilmes? What would they have to say about your claims of innocence?" At the mention of her fraud victims, she didn't pale as he'd expected her. Her confused look threw him off for a moment but he shelved it. "You played yourself false to those kindhearted people and you took all they had to fund your little East Coast excursion. Barbara and Winifred were old ladies and that's bad enough but the worst one, I think, was Isaac. You played him like a fiddle and left him not only broke but broken-hearted."

Something flitted across her face—guilt perhaps—but then she lifted her chin and responded with a quiet but unapologetic, "I told him I wasn't the marrying type. I never lied to him."

"Except the part where you lied about who you were, your past and the future you had no intention of sharing with him."

Her mouth tightened as her eyes narrowed. "I don't have to explain myself to you. My reasons were my own. Isaac has nothing to do with anything. Leaving someone isn't against the law."

"No, but representing yourself as someone you're not and getting someone to propose to you under false pretenses is called fraud."

"That's ridiculous. If that were the case every single person who's used their natural assets, be it a pretty face, big breasts, or money to get what they want would be guilty of fraud. And that's not what happened with Isaac, not that it's your business," she snapped. "I had feelings for him. Just not *those* kinds of feelings."

"You liked him enough to accept the four-carat diamond he put on your finger," he reminded her softly. "A diamond I suspect you sold the minute you left."

"It must be nice to be able to judge from that high horse of yours," she said. Then her mouth pinched in scorn as she added, "And for your information I sent that monstrosity back to him. I didn't want it in the first place but I hadn't wanted to humiliate him in front of his family and friends."

"So you left him at the altar?" he asked, incredulous. "That seems far more humiliating than just turning a man down when he's on bended knee."

"I was a fool to think you might be willing to listen to my side of things. You've obviously got your mind made up about me and what I've done." She started to back away and he shouted at her to wait but she was already fading into the darkness. Her voice floated back to him, taunting. "Look deeper, Tommy...look deeper."

And then she was gone.

THOMAS DIDN'T WANT TO admit it but Cassi's parting words had burrowed under his skin like a tiny sliver with the tip only partially exposed, too small to grab and pull out yet big enough to make him want to gouge it from his flesh. What had she meant, "look deeper"?

Damned if he knew but that's what he was doing, sitting in a cheap hotel, laptop open, reading her case file. Again.

At first glance it seemed pretty straightforward. Classic identity theft and fraud. But when he pulled the victim statements, he found one troubling similarity.

Their stories were nearly identical, which in itself

was no shock, especially if Cassi was using the same M.O. to achieve her goal. But the similarities in the statements were downright uncanny, as if they'd read a script and were delivering their lines. And the amounts lost seemed a helluva lot of money for two widows to have stockpiled. It wasn't impossible but…he scribbled a note to double-check the backgrounds of Barbara Hanks and Winifred Jones.

And then there was the expression on Cassi's face when he'd mentioned their names. She'd been genuinely shocked to hear that they'd pressed charges against her. Why would a woman who'd swindled two little old ladies be surprised by their decision to turn her in? Unless she hadn't done anything wrong in the first place…

He shook his head. No. God, he was being drawn into whatever illusion she'd spun for the victims. Classic mistake. Pretty girl, sad story of persecution…this was the kind of stuff they warned rookies about. But there was a troubling question that kept crowding his thoughts each time he tried to move forward. Why would two old women conspire and make false charges against Cassi? It was crazy. It wasn't his problem. Not his job to investigate, just to haul her in. But this was Cassi…how could he walk away with these unanswered questions in his head? They would drive him crazy.

He leaned over and grabbed his cell phone. He made a quick call to another agent. It was late but he knew this guy was still up. He was in the cyber crimes division and held late hours.

"D'Marcus, Thomas Bristol…you got a minute?" he asked, switching his Bluetooth on so he could talk with free use of his hands. "Can you do me a solid? I need a little help following up on a hunch."

"Glad to hear I'm not the only government employee still hard at work at such a ridiculous hour. What's the favor and before I say yes, what's in it for me, brother?"

Thomas grinned. "My sincere appreciation. I'd hate to think you're open to persuasion."

D'Marcus barked a short laugh. "Always the stickler for rules, man. All right, what's the favor?"

"I'm working on a case involving identity theft. Can you access the bank records of a Barbara Hanks and Winifred Jones?"

"You got their socials?"

"Yeah, gimme a minute," he said, scrolling to the victim page with their personal information. He gave the numbers and waited for D'Marcus to do his magic.

"So what am I looking for?" D'Marcus came back, a frown in his tone. "I don't see anything that jumps out as unusual. A lot of pharmacy runs…not so weird given they're both old ladies. Oh, ouch. Major withdrawal. About five thousand dollars. Brought Hanks's savings balance to zero. Same with the other chick. This the work of your suspect?"

"Yeah, so the report says," he murmured. "Any new accounts opened in the past month or so?"

There was a short pause while D'Marcus looked it up. Then, he said, "Actually, yeah…just the other day. Major deposits. Thirty thousand each. Damn. That's one heck of a payday."

He agreed. And highly irregular for two widowed ladies on modest pensions. "Where'd the money come from?" he asked.

"Looks like a wire transfer from a Swiss account. What the hell were these little old biddies into? Something seems a bit off."

"You got that right. Can you forward me the bank transcripts? I need to follow the trail."

"You got it, buddy."

"Thanks, D'Marcus."

"Happy to help. Hey, I heard you're the man for Celtics tickets?"

"It's true. I'm a fan." Thomas grinned. "I've been known to acquire a few tickets now and then when I want to get away. I went to college with a guy who now works in promotions for the team. He can always find a ticket for me when I want one. You need me to hook you up?"

"If you could manage it. I've got a girl who's crazy about basketball. Figured I should do it up right and take her to a game."

"Sounds like a keeper. Sure. I'll call my guy and have a few tickets set aside for the next home game."

"You're the best, Bristol."

Thomas clicked off and opened the file that D'Marcus sent. Obviously, these women weren't high-tech criminals. They hadn't tried—or known how—to hide money coming from the transfer, which would've been smart if they were getting a payoff for making a false report. He leaned back, lacing his fingers behind his head as he stretched, still in thought. A few soft and satisfying pops later, he was still mired in thoughts he had no business thinking but he knew he was going to make some phone calls first thing in the morning. The question was…what happened if the answers didn't point to Cassi's guilt, but rather her innocence?

It wasn't his call to tear into this investigation. His job had been to bring her in. Simple. Yet, he should've known nothing involving Cassi was going to end up simple and tidy. Her middle name should've been *complicated*.

He muttered under his breath. He knew he

couldn't walk away, hand over the case and forget about it.

And there was no sense in pretending that he could.

CASSI TOWEL-DRIED HER HAIR and then ran her fingers through it, looking for spots of blond through the Brunette Bombshell she'd picked up at the drugstore before checking into the cheap motel. She couldn't go sporting her natural color when the law was on her tail. The lush brown didn't do much for her complexion but she wasn't worried about winning any beauty pageants at the moment. She just wanted to pass by a cop without raising an eyebrow.

The need to yawn coincided with the fatigue pulling on her eyelids and, after tossing the brown-smudged towel on the floor, she climbed onto the bed and crawled under the cheap, scratchy comforter and tried not to think of when it had last been washed. For thirty-nine dollars a night, one couldn't expect the Ritz, but Cassi had a mild phobia about dirty linens after she'd watched a show on Discovery Channel about bedbugs and all sorts of creepy crawlies and bacteria that thrive in motel bedsheets. Not to mention the stuff that people—specifically couples—leave behind. She squeezed her eyes shut. *Don't think, just sleep.*

But she couldn't sleep. Images of Tommy bombarded her. Damn him anyway.

She could still see him, clutching the fence and imploring her with his eyes. Did he think she was going to roll over and quit just because he asked her to? Of all people, she'd held the tiniest hope, when she'd held none for anyone else, that Tommy would understand. He knew what it felt like to lose everything. If she had half a chance to prove that Lionel was a bad man she was going to take it. Her need to prove Lionel was a liar had ceased to be about money within the first six months. Actually, the minute she realized her need went deeper than money, was a blessing of clarity. She'd always considered herself unaffected by the fact that her family was ridiculously wealthy. She'd never held herself above anyone else because they had less, but it wasn't until she'd been thrust, penniless, onto the streets that she'd understood how foolish—no, arrogant—she'd been to think that she was like everyone else.

That first night, crouched shivering in a gas stop bathroom, using the hand blower for her stinging fingers…she'd known then how far from real life she'd been. For crap's sake, she hadn't even been able to work a washing machine. A maid had always whisked away her dirty clothes and replaced them— clean and folded or pressed, whatever the case may be—back in her dresser or closet. She hadn't thought about the process or considered that she could screw up a load of laundry and end up ruining the only clothes she'd been able to grab before getting tossed out on her ear. She discovered the value of a dollar— before she'd never given price a thought. That first trip to the grocery store had been an enlightening experience. It's hard to stretch five measly dollars, but when it's all you have in the world, you learn real fast how to make it work. And sometimes the only way to make it work is to employ the five-finger discount.

A groan threatened to surface and she hugged the flat, slightly odd-smelling pillow to her face. Tommy had no idea what kind of guilt she suffered for the morals she'd had to compromise simply to stay alive. There were things in her mental lockbox that she'd never dare let anyone see. It was bad enough they were stashed in her head forever. There wasn't enough cleanser on the planet to bleach the stain of what she'd done from her brain. There was nothing romantic about homelessness. Anyone who said anything different was on drugs.

But even though she was far from that scared homeless young woman, there were times when she resurfaced, frightened and vulnerable. Tonight was one of those times.

She tried to let her mind go blank, welcoming the

exhaustion so that she could forget about the events of the day, but even as she slipped into dreamland, Tommy wasn't far from her thoughts.

Even in the wispy landscape of her dreams…he followed.

She'd been slightly tipsy. A party at her house while her parents were away had gotten a little wild. Of course, Tommy had come because he rarely disappointed her by declining her requests, but the minute he'd seen the people acting like a bunch of drunken idiots, his face had darkened and her only thought had been to keep him from leaving.

For some reason it had mattered to her that he stayed.

"Stay. Have some fun, Tommy," she'd pleaded, her voice bordering on playfulness. When had Tommy Bristol become such a cutie? Had she never noticed the firm swell of young muscle in his biceps or how the stubborn tightness of his jaw when he was pissed made him look…delicious?

"Cassi, these people aren't your friends. They're just using you for your money," he'd said, raining on her buzz.

She'd frowned. "That's not nice. Of course they're my friends. Well, all except her." She'd pointed not so discreetly at Monica Kriek, whom she actually scowled at. Who had invited her anyway, she started to mutter, but Tommy had grabbed her arm and pulled her to a quiet spot away from the crowd. "What are you doing? Oh, good, I needed some fresh air…"

"Cassi, I'm not staying," he said, and she was shocked to see disappointment in his eyes. "I just came to give you this as an early birthday gift because I won't be able to make your actual birthday." He placed a small box in her hand, tied neatly with a simple purple bow, her favorite color. "I hope you like it."

Curious, and delighted at the prospect of a gift, she opened the box. A silver locket lay nestled within the tissue. She lifted the fine chain and popped the little door on the locket. A picture of him and her when they were young stared back at her. She sobered as she stared at the picture. She remembered the day quite clearly. She'd taken it the first day they'd ever met. She'd been playing with her new camera and had been drawn to the boy in the park who'd looked so sad it made her heart hurt just to look at him.

"How did you get this?" she asked quietly.

"I found the original in your room and had a smaller copy made," he admitted. "I managed to return the original before you noticed it was missing."

Her mouth had tipped in a warm smile. "You little thief," she murmured, though in truth she'd been inordinately touched by the gift. It was her favorite picture. "I love it." She stepped forward to give him a hug but as his arms closed around her, she didn't feel the comfort of familiarity. Instead, a zing of awakening awareness caused her to see Tommy with fresh eyes filled with wonder and tingles cascading through her body at the contact. Her heart hammered in her chest and her arms wound around his neck as if they were made to fit there. Her mouth angled toward his, and a wild, almost scared thought raced through her mind—*Are you really about to kiss Tommy Bristol? Your best friend in the world?*—before she closed the distance and felt his mouth move against hers. Their tongues touched in a tentative, explorative motion that sent need and desire hurtling through her body. She wasn't prepared for what it meant and the devastation that could occur if it all went to crap. She pulled away, desperate to put space between them and her feelings. "I truly love the gift," she said, her voice husky and raw. "But I have to get back to the party. Thank you…"

And as she melted into the crowd, eager for another beer to drown what she couldn't deal with, she cast one last glance Tommy's way but he was gone.

THOMAS ROSE EARLY, ROLLING from his bed before the sun crested the horizon, and was showered and dressed just as the first rays started caressing the frozen landscape.

By 8:00 a.m. he was packed and ready to leave. The lack of restful sleep—the bed had more lumps than poorly cooked Cream of Wheat—left his eyes gritty and stinging in the face of the harsh morning light, but he was too focused on finding the answers he sought to worry about anything else.

He had to find Cassi and he held little hope that he'd be able to find her without some assistance.

First, he dialed the bus station where he'd lost her. He knew she wouldn't use her real name but perhaps she'd used the identity she'd been using in New York.

The gravelly voice of a ticket agent who wasn't a fan of mornings picked up the line. He identified himself and he could've sworn he could hear the agent's disinterest over the phone.

"I'm looking for information on a ticket purchased by a suspect possibly going by the name Trinity Moon. Do you have anything in your database with that name?"

There was a short pause and the clack of the woman's nails on the keyboard, then, "No."

"How about Cassi Nolan?" he tried.

Another pause, followed by a bored, "No."

"Try Cassandra Nolan."

"Are we going to do this all day? I've got a line growing," she complained.

"We could. Or I could chat with your supervisor about your customer service skills and if that doesn't faze you, how about I just have you brought in for obstruction of justice?"

She grumbled but snapped, "What's the other name?"

He thought a minute. What name would Cassi use that wouldn't be an easy connection? Something only someone close to her might guess.... His mind picked over and skimmed ideas but nothing hit him right away. He was almost ready to give up when his thoughts took a different route. "Try Amy Anderson," he suggested, hoping the hunch panned out.

"What do you know, there is an Amy Anderson ticket purchased two months ago and used last night. Is that all?"

"Destination?"

"Newark, New Jersey."

He smiled. "Thanks for your help."

"Sure." The withering response came as he hung up. Nothing like a New York public servant to brighten an early morning.

Why Newark? No matter. He had her secret name. This was likely the name she used as a blank slate before she created her next identity. He didn't know why he didn't think of it before. Now he could track her as easily as following a light in the dark.

CHAPTER SIX

MAMA JO'S MIND WAS FULL of odds and ends—
which in itself wasn't unusual—but there was something lurking at the edge of her thoughts that made
her want to do a double check over her shoulder for
shadows.

She adjusted the shawl over her thin shoulders and
surveyed her hands with the critical eye of someone
who'd seen a lot and done even more. She was getting old. Even if her mind was still sharp, her body
was giving little signals and signs that she was no
longer twenty-five.

She ambled outside, shivering as the winter air
invaded her bones, and made quick work of grabbing
an armful of wood to bring back inside.

Was it so long ago that her foster boys once ran
amok in the little farmhouse? Was it even longer
that her own boy died? The breath hitched in her
chest for a painful moment and she waited for it to
pass. Ah, Cordry, she thought on a sigh. Would he
have grown to be a better man than he had been as
a misled teen? Only God knew for sure. She tried

not to dwell on the past but there were ghosts in the house it seemed.

She remembered his smile, fleeting though it was, and his love for strawberry pancakes. The rest of the details of his thirteen-year-old life were fading from her memory, slipping into a fuzzy void that sucked up the moments that gave her pain. And that's how it should be, she realized. There was little that could be done to change the past. She knew that better than anyone and she tried to pass that on to her foster boys; Lord knew they needed to hold that lesson to their hearts. Bless them, each had been given a rough row to hoe.

A knock at the door interrupted her musings and revealed a man she'd never seen and would've figured for a salesman if not for his fine clothes and fancy wheels parked out front. Still, she had no desire for company at the moment so she attempted to shoo him along.

"Sorry, son, you're barking up the wrong tree here. Ain't nothing in the cookie jar but a few crumbs these days," she said, moving to close the door. He stopped her with an apologetic expression.

"Excuse me, Ms. Bell, for intruding on this fine winter day but I obtained information that you once knew my daughter," he said as his mouth tipped in a disarming smile that Mama Jo didn't trust one bit.

She narrowed her stare at him, and he hastened to add, "I'm Lionel Vissher. My daughter is Cassandra Nolan."

"You mean your *stepdaughter,* don't you, because I remember her father and you ain't him."

His mouth turned down. "Yes, of course. Step-daughter. Do you by any chance know where she is? I heard at one time she used to be very close to your foster son and spent a lot of time here in your house."

The way he said it made her feel as if she'd transgressed for allowing a young girl to find solace and companionship at her hearth. She tightened her shawl around her shoulders but didn't invite the man in. She'd rather stand there and shiver to death than give this Lionel character any comfort. Mama Jo found him distasteful and didn't mind letting it show in her expression. She didn't know where Cassi was but even if she did, she doubted she'd share that information with this man. His eyes were flinty and cold even if he was going out of his way to appear harmless. "It's been a long time since Cassi Nolan spent any time in this house," she said, leaving it at that.

And a pity, too. She cared for that girl and hoped she came to her senses sooner rather than later, but Thomas hadn't mentioned her name once since their big blowup all those years ago in college. Mama Jo had hoped—well, shoot, if you twisted her arm she'd admit she'd prayed—that those two were going to tie the knot someday. Alas, she thought on a private sigh, it hadn't worked out that way.

"Yes, well, she hasn't been home in a long time, either," he admitted. "I just worry. I'd like to know she's all right. You know, I'm her only family since her mother's passing two years ago. I'd feel better if I at least knew where she was, even if she didn't want to come home. Surely, as a mother, you understand my feelings." She grunted something in agreement and he took that as a positive sign and handed her a business card. "If she contacts you…please let me know. I would be most appreciative, Ms. Bell. Perhaps," he said slyly as he walked away. "I could even make it worth your while."

'Coon poop, that's what he was. She recognized a bribe when she saw it. She watched as he climbed into that ridiculous-looking fancy car that was ill-suited for her country road and when he'd disappeared, she went inside and ripped the card to pieces before tossing it into the fire along with a fresh log. If he wanted to find Cassi, he could do it himself. She wasn't about to tattle on the girl. If she wanted to come home, she would.

Mama Jo settled in her favorite chair to warm her frozen bones and her thoughts wandered to Thomas. A smile followed. The strong, silent one with the biggest heart—a heart that had only ever belonged to one person...and that girl had been too silly to notice.

Well, maybe that would change. She could only hope. An all-over fatigue wore her out, and she closed her eyes. Seemed the need to nap came more and more when before she'd managed on a handful of hours. Growing boys had needed constant super-vision. A few minutes of shut-eye sounded just the thing...and then she'd make some chili, because nothing tasted better on a cold day than hot chili.

CASSI LOCKED HER MOTEL room door, the sharp smell of hair dye still fresh in her nose, and set out for the public library. She was short on funds; and she needed access to a computer. The public library—particularly those of big cities—offered free internet access as well as a convenient place to spend a few hours crafting a new identity. If anyone asked, she could easily pull off the lit grad student excuse, always taking care to have a few classics in her book pile.

She hailed a taxi and stared out the window, glancing at the skyline with a sigh. A storm broiled, kicking up dark ominous clouds that promised snow before the end of the day, and she shivered against the chill coming from the finger-smudged glass. She hadn't planned to use that bus ticket to Newark until the spring. "Damn you, Tommy," she muttered before closing her eyes.

The details of downtown Newark were lost on her, but she wasn't there to sightsee anyway. For the past two years she'd appreciated little of the places she'd traveled. It wasn't until about six months ago that she'd finally stumbled across a piece of information that was truly useful in her search. There were days she'd lost hope of finding anything. She supposed she had Isaac to thank for the discovery.

Poor Isaac. She felt more than a twinge of guilt for the part she played in his inevitable heartbreak. She shifted in her seat, her mouth tightening at the contempt she'd heard in Tommy's voice at her deception of Isaac. He didn't have all the facts. How dare he judge her? She'd broken no law with Isaac but she had used him for information. Her cheeks burned at the private admission. She'd tried to warn him—in her own way. She'd never actually said, *Isaac, don't fall in love with me because I'm only using you for your connections,* but she had told him that she wasn't the marrying type. Perhaps she should've found another way. Another sigh escaped her and she tightened her grip on her pack. There'd been no other way. But when things were returned to normal she swore to apologize to Isaac, to explain. Just as she would explain to everyone she'd crossed paths with under a false identity. And yes, she knew there were many who deserved a profuse apology at the least.

But that wasn't today.

Cassi paid the taxi driver and ascended the stairs of the three-story building. It stood sentinel on the street, imposing its shadow and wearing its age like a distinguished gentleman. It was a shame she wasn't here to admire the architecture.

Perhaps one of these days…

THOMAS FOUND THE MOTEL EASILY. The greasy clerk—a man who looked as if he wouldn't bat an eye at renting out a room by the hour—gave up the room key the minute Thomas flashed the badge. Not that he expected anything to the contrary. He found most people who didn't want too much attention on themselves were more than happy to direct that attention elsewhere.

"I run a legitimate business here," the clerk called out, the higher pitch of his tone betraying his nerves. "I ain't harboring no fugitives. That's a fact."

"Thanks for your help," Thomas said in a low growl. Then added, "If I find you tipped her off in any way, I'll see that this place is crawling with feds before you can get out of town. If there's even a hair out of place on your record, I'll ream you for it."

The clerk gulped and made a gesture of zipping his lips.

"That's what I thought."

Thomas let himself into the room and locked it again behind him. He did a quick search to ensure she wasn't there and when he was satisfied he was quite alone in the cramped, unattractive, and only marginally clean room, he took a seat and prepared to wait.

IT WAS DARK AND BITTER COLD by the time she returned to the motel. The chocolate-brown woolen scarf wound around her neck did little to stop the cold from seeping into her bones. Her fingers were nearly numb—the thin gloves weren't sufficient for the kind of windchill cutting around the buildings—and all she could focus on was getting the key in the lock and escaping the freezing snow that was about to fall any minute.

She closed the door behind her and flexed her frozen fingers as she tossed the key to the small table barely illuminated by the glow peeping around the closed drapes and fumbled with the light switch. Weak, watery light bathed the room and she turned, nearly swallowing her tongue at the sight of Tommy sitting on her bed, his gun pointing straight at her heart. *Aunt Jemima pancakes!* She startled and flattened herself against the door, her hand instinctively going for the knob, but at Tommy's hardened stare she didn't even try to turn it and slowly dropped her hand.

"I give you props for ingenuity but demerits for dumping my car and making me file a stolen vehicle report. Nice color, by the way," he said, referencing her new brunette style. "What? Did you get tired of blond jokes?"

"Who doesn't get tired of those," she countered, her mind working so fast her thoughts were beginning to blur. "I thought a change was in order."

"Especially since your face and physical characteristics were going to be plastered on every precinct wall on the eastern seaboard."

She offered him a small smile. "Well, there was that. Sorry about the car. I couldn't very well hang on to it. All government vehicles are equipped with GPS tracking devices," she managed to retort with a modicum of calm that she certainly didn't feel. Tommy was pointing a gun at her. And judging by the mean-eyed, cold stare he was giving her…he just might pull the trigger. "How did you find me?" she asked.

"Given your propensity for slipping out of my custody I think I'll keep that information to myself just in case it happens again."

She worried her bottom lip as she ran through her own checklist of possibilities. Then, she thought of the name she used to register the room, and when she swore under her breath he knew she'd figured it out.

He smirked. "Amy Anderson. A. A. I always thought it was a little weird that you used your mom's Alcoholics Anonymous code name as your fake identity when we were kids."

She glowered. Her mom hadn't been able to admit she was an alcoholic so she'd invented the fictitious Amy Anderson as the friend she'd visit each week when she'd attend her meetings. It was perverse and it was private. She hated that Tommy remembered such a small detail about her life. She lifted her chin. "Yeah? So?"

He chuckled, but the sound didn't have anything in common with laughter. He waved the gun at her. "Take a seat. We need to chat."

Should she run? No. It was now snowing outside. She had no transportation, sparse funds, and he clearly had the upper hand. She cautiously lowered herself to the chair beside the table and took a moment to assess the situation.

"Toss me that key, would you?" It wasn't a request, it was a demand. She did as he asked. He caught it with a twist of his wrist, the hand holding the gun never wavering from its target. "Now, about that chat," he began, and she started to tell him that he needn't bother, but he wasn't about to let her get a word in. He shushed her with an expletive and a scowl that sent electricity arcing down to her toes. She'd never seen Tommy so angry, so bristling with a dark energy that alternately pulled and repelled. He'd always been the calm one, the guy who could always mellow the storm. Now he was creating one. Her breathing quickened along with her blood. She curled her fingers into fists, digging her nails into her palm to clear her mind. She withheld the wince but the pain served its purpose. "Let's start from the beginning," he instructed.

"Why?" she asked, stalling. "You aren't interested in my side of the story."

He ignored that and moved on as if she hadn't spoken. "At first I was pretty sure you were like every other felon, lying to further your own gain, but you were damn desperate to get to that book I suspect you've got in your pack. So that made me wonder, what's in the book that you're willing to go back to New York to fetch, knowing that would be the first place I'd go looking for you. So, against my better judgment, I started doing a little extra work. I looked into your file. I went deeper." He paused and she held her breath, not daring to believe. "And I found some irregularities."

"Such as?" she asked, watching him intently. Was it too much to hope that he'd seen enough to question her guilt? Was it enough to gain an ally? Someone she could trust? The hope alone was cruel.

"Perhaps we could trade notes. I've found irregularities myself. But maybe you could lower the gun? I have an aversion to guns being pointed at my heart."

"That depends. I already know I can't trust you so what assurances do I have that you're not going to bolt the minute I do?"

"You don't. You've already stated that you can't trust me and given my track record that's a fairly accurate assessment. But trust is a leap of faith. So, the question is, do you take that leap or continue to hold on to what you know has happened before?"

"Yes, that is the question," he agreed softly, his eyes never leaving hers. After a long moment, he blew a short breath and finally lowered the gun. "Fine," he said, placing the gun with deliberate caution on the nightstand. "But don't try anything, Cassi. You've used up all your credit with me."

And he meant it. She suppressed a shiver but she put on a show of bravery. "Don't be so melodramatic, Tommy. Where am I going to go? In case you haven't noticed, it's snowing outside and I used public transit to get here."

"That brings us to a puzzling question…why here? Newark? Did you just pick a place on the map for kicks?"

"Of course not. But to answer that I'd have to

assume that you truly care about the truth and what I'm after."

"And if I do?"

"Then you'd have to believe that I'm innocent."

"Are you?"

"Yes." *Mostly.* But no sense in confusing the issue. She was innocent of the most serious crimes and that's what mattered at the moment. "Are you ready to hear my side?"

"I'm sitting here, aren't I?"

She made a face. "So grouchy."

"Pardon me. I tend to get a little less happy when I'm forced to chase a suspect all over creation. You have no idea the ass-reaming I'm going to get over this...not to mention the paperwork."

"Sorry to complicate your life," she said, not quite able to keep the sarcasm from her voice. "Try being on the run for the past two years. Imagine the inconvenience of not knowing where you're going to lay your head at night."

Silence sat between them and she wished she'd kept that last comment to herself. It made her sound pathetic and vulnerable.

"Cassi...you could've called me before it got to this stage," he said quietly, though the admission seemed to take effort, as if it were pulled out of him.

She looked away, unable to bear the look in his

eyes. "No, I couldn't," she answered, leaving it at that. She'd tried to find him but they'd lost contact with one another and she'd been too ashamed to call Mama Jo. She'd assumed Tommy had told his foster mother some of the things she'd said when they'd parted ways. Her cheeks burned just to remember the foul things that had come out of her mouth when she'd been too hopped up on coke to care who she hurt. "I didn't know who I could trust. You, included. I couldn't take the chance. Looks like I wasn't wrong. Here you are…ready to bundle me up and deliver me like a Christmas turkey."

"So you're the victim here?" he countered, the edge returning to his voice.

"I didn't say that…exactly. But I'm not the criminal you think I am."

He shook his head, the small movement saying *I'm tired and don't want to get involved but I will anyway* and she caught a glimmer of opportunity. Buried deep under layers of time was the affection he'd once felt for her. She sensed it, even if he was trying to smother it under the weight of duty. If she could coax that piece of him to the surface…she might find a way out of this.

"Prove it," he challenged, his gaze searching hers, as if looking for something to hold on to even if he didn't want to find it.

She couldn't trust him, but God, yes, there was a

part of her that wanted to lay everything at his feet, to unburden herself of the load she'd been carrying…but she couldn't. Tommy was an FBI agent, not her friend. However, she could pretend to trust him to get him to loosen up. She offered him a tentative smile. "Just do me one small favor…" He awaited her request, his gaze narrowing as if he were bracing himself. She looked away, allowing her embarrassment to show through as she said, "And there's no need to point out that you've got the upper hand and I'm in no shape to be calling in favors." He grunted something in agreement and she drew a short breath for strength, for her newest plan was the worst she'd ever put together. She was fairly certain if she managed to pull it off, she was going to hell because it would destroy the one thing she'd always held sacred in her heart. Her eyes met his and held. "Promise me we'll stay here for the night and you'll hear me out."

Tommy stared, as if trying to guess her game. "I'm sure the roads are clear. You talk, I'll drive."

"I know I don't deserve it but I need you to hear me out. *If,* after you've heard everything and you still believe taking me to the authorities is the best course of action, I will go without a fight. I promise. *Please,* Tommy." She implored him as much with her eyes as with her tone as she cautiously approached him. When all he did was stiffen but didn't reach for his gun, she gathered more courage and knelt between his legs, her hands sliding up his thigh, testing. His muscles tensed under her palms as she looked up at him, uttering the words she never thought she'd say to her best friend under these circumstances. She hoped it worked. "Stay with me tonight."

THOMAS JERKED AT THE implication in her eyes and the heat radiating from her hands. Anyone else and they'd never have even gotten this far. But oddly, he'd been dry-mouth curious about where she was going with this. He'd thought he could take whatever she was trying to serve him but now, with her so close he could smell her skin, her lips parting in invitation, he was fighting a part of himself that should've been quiet and docile.

Instead, it had roared to life. He swallowed but held his ground. Perhaps he'd see how far she was willing to take things. He glanced down at her hand, inching closer to the heated apex of his thighs. "Careful," he murmured, his voice close to a growl. "You could get yourself into a lot of trouble."

"I'm already in trouble," she said, inching her hand farther. "What's a little more?"

CHAPTER SEVEN

TOMMY REACHED AROUND HER, one arm sliding behind her waist to pull her close. She inhaled sharply and her eyes flared wide but she didn't retreat. Her tongue snaked out to tease her bottom lip and he was too caught up in the moment to remember that he was trying to call her bluff. And that moment was scorching. All the years he'd told himself his childhood crush was over, that Cassi was nothing more than a placeholder in his memory for the real deal that would come later, he knew he'd been fooling himself. Cassi was here, warm and alive, pressed against him and he was struggling to recall who was supposed to be in control.

The seventeen-year-old Thomas Bristol who should've been long gone, awoke from a deep sleep and took over.

"This is too easy," he murmured, his skin tingling where her hands rested against his chest. "You can't think that I don't see what you're doing, and it's beneath you, Cassi."

She jerked, her gaze narrowing but he held her

tight. "Let me go then," she demanded, losing the softness he saw only moments prior. Her muscles rigid, she pushed against him but he had the advantage. It wasn't right for him to continue to hold her like this but he'd be a liar if he said he didn't get an illicit enjoyment from it. "You've made your point. Now get your hands off me before I start screaming my head off."

"Go ahead," he taunted her. "You're in my custody and I've already shown the clerk my badge. As far as he's concerned, you're not his problem."

Her mouth pinched but her cheeks flared with high heat. She was fighting mad and it only made her sexier. Damn, and he wasn't immune to the effect she had on him. His jeans started to tighten and he realized he may have lost his edge in this fight but he couldn't let her know that.

She must've sensed something for her expression turned cunning and she angled her head to regard him with that turbulent gaze of hers. Instead of struggling against him, she turned the tables and slid her hands around his neck.

"Oh, Tommy," she murmured, her sweet voice sliding like something naughty across his nerve endings. "You're not so tough, you know. I know all your secrets. Your weak spots. I know you want me…always have. And here I am. All yours. Don't you want a taste?"

He swallowed what felt like his Adam's apple and he tried to set her away from him, but she clung to him like a spider monkey, pressing herself against him in all the right spots. "Okay, knock it off," he demanded, but his voice betrayed a subtle tremble. His hands ached to explore the curves of her plump ass as his tongue plunged into her mouth and other places. He was holding on to his resolve by the thinnest of threads. "Damn it, Cassi, you're messing with fire. You don't want to do this."

She laughed, low and throaty, and rubbed herself against him, her breath hitching in her throat before whispering against the shell of his ear, "You're always trying to tell me what to do. I see some things haven't changed."

Like hell they hadn't. At that, he managed to set her away from him, his breathing labored, his heart banging hard against his chest as if he'd run a marathon. He narrowed his stare at her as she watched him with a knowing smirk. "Is this all a game to you?" he asked, pissed at himself and at her for trying something so stupid. "I'm an FBI agent here to arrest you. Don't you realize what kind of trouble you're in? I could drag your ass in right now and be done with it but you've got me asking questions I shouldn't give a shit about and here you're still playing me like I'm some ordinary jerk who doesn't know you from Eve. You're right—you know some of my secrets but, honey, you've forgotten…I know all of *yours*."

The smirk dissolved from her expression and he saw something flit across her features, chased by a brief moment of vulnerability and aching loneliness, and he almost felt bad for her. But, damn it, she brought this on herself.

Her eyes glittered but she held back the tears and for that, he was grateful. Cassi crying was more than he could handle at the moment. "Fine," she conceded, moving to the chair, her expression turning mutinous. "You've made your point. Abundantly. So now what?"

It would've been a simple thing to close the short distance between his lips and hers but he couldn't do it. As shamefully as he wanted to taste her on his tongue, he wouldn't. Not like this. He was in a position of authority and he'd never abuse that power.

He sighed, feeling quite distinctly that he'd just cut her pride cleanly in half, but knew he'd made the right choice—even if his libido was screaming something different. He resigned himself to a difficult evening. "Now, you tell me your side of things. And please, just stick to the facts. No embellishing or deleting in your favor. I need to know it all, even if it's not pretty. Can you do that?"

THE BACK OF CASSI'S THROAT ached as tears threatened to demolish the rest of her battered ego but a

part of her was sagging with relief. If Tommy had…
if he'd allowed her to seduce him, her respect for
him would've died a messy death, and above all
else, what made Tommy special was his backbone.
He never caved under peer pressure, never felt compelled to do as the others were doing if it didn't jibe
with his internal gauge and she'd respected the hell
out of that. So, *yay!* for intestinal fortitude but *ouch*
for her self-esteem. She tucked her knees into the
cradle of her arms and wondered how much to share,
how much to edit. She drew a deep breath. "Where
should I start?" she asked.

"Start from the point when you went on the run.
I pretty much know the story before that."

He was referencing her party days. He knew because that's when she'd kicked him out of her life.
She was tempted to offer an apology for her ap-
palling behavior back then, but she didn't see the
purpose except easing her own guilt so she kept it
to herself.

"Ah, well, let's see…my dad died about five years
after we graduated high school," she started, surprised by the sudden sting of tears even after all this
time.

"I'm sorry about your dad," he offered gruffly,
and she accepted the sentiment with a nod. "Mama
Jo told me but…"

"I know…we weren't exactly on speaking terms.

Don't worry about it. I won't hold that against you."
She had plenty to hold against him aside from that
painful moment in her past, starting with his decision to treat her like a criminal. Refocusing, she
continued, "My mom met Lionel Vissher about three
years after that. He seemed nice enough…I mean,
my mom and I weren't really getting along all because of the crowd I was running with. I got into
some trouble. Nothing major," she clarified a bit
defensively. "Mostly misdemeanors."

"Mostly?"

She looked away. "Yeah. Mostly."

"I'd call a felony DUI pretty major," he said, and
she turned to stare at him. Of course he'd read her
file and that particular episode was on her permanent record.

"Yes, it is. And I never did it again. Please don't
lecture me."

He held his hands up in a conciliatory gesture.
"No lecture. Just statement of fact. But I do find
it interesting that you tend to gloss over the parts
where you're in the wrong."

She stiffened. "I'm not glossing over anything. I
know I screwed up. I paid my dues. And I learned
my lesson," she said. "May I continue?"

"Please do. I'm still waiting for the part where
you prove that you're the innocent one. So far…I'm
not convinced."

She didn't snap at the bait but she did communicate her feelings with a healthy glare sent his way. So self-righteous. Like Tommy Bristol never made a mistake? She choked back the hot words bubbling to the surface. Lord, her temper would be the death of her. She drew a deep breath before continuing. "Like I said, at first Lionel seemed an all right guy. I mean, he wasn't my dad, that's for sure, but there wasn't anyone who would've measured up. I tried not to let that influence me, though, but maybe it did. But whatever…my mom was really taken with him and he made her happy. It wasn't until later when I realized he was siphoning money from various accounts that I started to get suspicious."

"How'd you find out he was doing that?"

"Complete accident. I went into my mom's office to find something on her computer and he'd left a browser open on the computer. It was a bank account in his name only at a bank I'd never heard of. My family has banked at the same bank for decades and I know my mom would never switch. She liked the preferential treatment they always gave her when she went into the local branch. I felt like I'd peeked into something that was none of my business and I felt bad so I almost closed the window but curiosity got the better of me—" she shrugged, not really sorry at all "—and I realized he'd been stockpiling money."

"Did you confront him about it?"

"Not at first. I was hoping I was wrong. I mean, I didn't want to make a wild accusation without some kind of proof and I wasn't sure I wanted to know the truth, either. My mom was really happy for once and I thought, maybe it's not a big deal in the overall scheme of things. But, in the end, I couldn't keep it going. Especially when he was spending my family's fortune on extravagant purchases, like yachts and parties—none of which my mom authorized."

"How do you know?"

"First, my mom hated the water. Boats scared her. That's why my dad never bought a yacht. He respected her fear and didn't want to make it worse. Second, my mom always seemed to find out about the parties after they were over. As in, he always seemed to forget to invite his own wife."

"I'll give you that he seems like an inconsiderate jerk but…"

"I'm not finished. That was just the beginning. I started asking around. I heard a rumor that he was messing around behind my mom's back. A maid heard Lionel in the bedroom with another woman while my mom was out shopping. I told my mom what I'd been told. At first she didn't want to believe me but I know I planted a seed of doubt because they started fighting. This went on for a while. I could tell my mom was under a huge strain but she tried to hide it. She even went so far as to give him lavish gifts but it felt desperate to me. Of course, she denied it. But…then she started getting sick."

"Sick?"

"Yeah." Her voice hitched with remembered pain. "At first, it was stomachaches. Real bad ones. But she'd get better and it was forgotten. Then they'd start again. She went to doctor after doctor and had gobs of tests done but everything always came up clean. The doctor said it was stress and suggested she start taking yoga or gardening."

"I remember your mom being a little high-strung…."

"She was, which didn't help matters. And neither did Lionel. I started asking questions and that's when he'd whisk her away for some kind of rejuvenating vacation, and funny enough, she always got better. Except when she came home, then it would start all over."

"No one thought that was odd?" he asked.

"Oh, yes. Lionel himself brought in all these specialists to test for *toxic mold,* and of course, the house came up clean but he put on a good show of really worrying about my mom's health."

"So what made you think he was the cause of her decline?"

She drew a deep breath, hating that she had so little to prove her theory, yet she knew in her heart that he had killed her mother. She shrugged. "Nothing really. Just a feeling."

"What did the autopsy say?"

"Because the police didn't suspect foul play, an autopsy wasn't done, and Lionel didn't ask for one."

"You could've pressed for it as a family member, particularly since you had concerns."

"By that point, Lionel had convinced the police that I was simply a disgruntled, spoiled brat who was just trying to create a distraction from my own problems."

"Was it true?" he asked carefully, and her head shot up. He lifted his hands. "I have to ask. The last time we spoke you were running with a party crowd that was into some serious shit."

The temptation to lie was great. She hated admitting what a mess she'd been. Tommy awaited an answer, but she couldn't mislead him, even to soften the rough edges of the truth. "I was messed up," she admitted. "But by the time my mom died I'd cleaned up. I'd stopped hanging around the party scene and I was trying to protect my mom. But she was fighting me as much as Lionel was trying to cover everything up. She couldn't believe that she was in danger. She thought the same thing Lionel was telling everyone else…that I was a spoiled brat trying to ruin my mom's life by making wild accusations. My record

didn't help. I didn't have anyone to turn to for help."
She was horrified to find her eyes welling and she
turned away so Tommy didn't catch it.

But it was too late. "Cassi," he called her name
softly. She reluctantly met his gaze. "Come here,"
he instructed.

"Why?"

"Just do it."

"A minute ago you said—"

"I know what I said. Just come here."

"When'd you get so bossy," she grumbled, but she
slowly closed the distance between them. In spite of
the circumstances, her heart rate kicked up a beat
just being so near to him. She didn't want to be this
close to him without a purpose or plan to put into
play. This felt real and was something she'd thought
of many times when she'd been cold, hungry and
lost, yet her pride and fear had kept her from picking
up the phone. "You don't want to do this, remember?" she said, her voice a husky whisper.

"I never said I didn't want to…I said I wouldn't,"
he corrected her, his hands at her waist drawing her
to him.

"What's the difference?" she asked. The wild,
intense heat in his eyes turned her knees to jelly,
and a shake had begun to steal the strength from
her legs. Her hands came to rest on his shoulders for

support as much as anything else, for she felt ready to slide to the floor.

"The difference is now you're being sincere. You're not playing an angle to get something from me."

"How do you know?" she said.

"Because I can see it in your eyes and hear it in your voice. Whatever you're feeling right now is real and it hurts."

God, he was right. Damn him for knowing her so well even after all these years. His next statement nearly did her in.

"Cassi, I would've been there for you. Despite all that'd been said between us, I would've dropped everything to help you. You have to know that, right?"

"No, I don't know that," she lied, blinking away the hot moisture. She swallowed. "I don't know that now."

His mouth tightened with displeasure at her continued mulishness but he seemed to understand where it was coming from. "I would've done whatever I could to help you. I promise you."

"What does it matter? I didn't come to you and I made my bed, right?"

"Cassi…"

"I don't need you to save me," she snapped bitterly. "I'm doing just fine on my own."

His arched brow said he didn't agree but her pride

had its demands and she couldn't say otherwise. They were in a standoff and Cassi didn't expect his next request so when it came she was caught off guard.

"I'm here for you now. Will you trust me?"

Time stopped with that single, loaded question. Trust him? She couldn't trust anyone. She had a price on her head and there was a man who would stop at nothing to keep his secret. But this was Tommy asking the question and she wanted to say yes. She wanted to simply nod and allow him to fix this problem. It was weak and sad and when this whole mess started she swore she'd never put herself in a situation where she felt either of those things. Yet, here she was…staring into the eyes of the man she should've been smart enough to marry, and content to have his babies—but she hadn't. She'd been stupid and hurtful and…naive about her place in the world and so had lost everything that had ever mattered. "I…" *Want to. Desperately.* But the truth was…she didn't know how to trust any longer. She was caught in a permanent cycle of fight or flight and she didn't know how to respond to something outside of those parameters. She couldn't tell him that, either. She ran the tip of her tongue along her bottom lip and Tommy's gaze fastened on the movement with an expression that was feral and achingly delicious, and she answered the only way she could, given the circumstances. "Yes, Tommy," she said. "I trust you."

Even if it was a total lie.

CHAPTER EIGHT

THOMAS'S HEART THRILLED at her words and relief followed, even if it was short-lived. He pushed away the grim leer of reality, knowing deep down that the odds were slim that she was telling the truth, but he so wanted to believe her. He wanted her to be innocent of the charges leveled against her, he wanted to believe that there was a very good reason for the things she'd done.

But at the moment, he wanted to savor whatever was happening between them.

She leaned into him and he allowed the gentle pressure to take them both down on the bed. She was lying with her leg thrown across his thighs with her head propped up by her elbow. "So what now?" she asked, gazing at him, waiting.

"In what context?" he countered.

She smiled. "In the context where I'm sprawled on top of you and we're both—" she glanced down at the obvious bulge in his jeans "—interested in seeing what happens next."

He reached over and smoothed her brown hair,

tucking it behind her ear. He'd always loved her golden hair but she looked pretty good as a brunette, too. There'd been many times he imagined this moment but it had never felt like this. He could smell the sweet scent of her skin, her hair and that unique blend that was just her. It was branded into his memory. Had he ever hoped to find someone else to replace her in his heart and mind? He'd been a fool to think he could do this job and not be affected. He wanted her so badly his teeth ached but there were rules, and if he was going to find a way to help her, he had to keep the lines drawn. He closed his eyes briefly and prayed for strength, then gently disentangled himself from beneath her firm and inviting body.

"Oh, so I guess nothing is going to happen," she surmised, plainly disappointed. "I guess it's for the best. No sense in complicating things, right?"

"Yeah." He sat up and she scooted against the headboard and folded her arms across her chest. He paused, waiting for his head to clear enough to speak coherently. His hormones were still doing flybys in his brain. "It's already complicated," he said, earning a frown from Cassie. "I'm going to do what I can to help you figure this out but if we start sleeping together…I'm afraid…well, it's just a bad idea."

She nodded, but she still had that vulnerable vibe about her, as if she didn't know how to process the logic behind the rejection. "So, how are you going to help me?" she finally asked.

"Well," he started, relieved to focus on something relatively safe between them. He needed it to get his head on straight. "I've already made some calls to a friend and he's running down some information on those old ladies you *befriended* in Virginia. Seems both recently made some hefty deposits."

"I didn't steal from them," she said, her frown deepening. "I mean, I borrowed a little but not enough to put them in a bad spot."

"According to the file, both ladies claim you bilked them out of their savings four months ago, which came to about five thousand dollars apiece." At her stunned expression, he decided either she was an amazing liar or she was truly shocked at the news. "But a few days ago, each one deposited thirty thousand dollars. Did either of them have family who might've left them an inheritance?"

Cassi thought for a moment then shrugged. "I don't know. I didn't get to know them that well. I was chasing down a lead and they were nice to me. Basically, I borrowed about five hundred dollars from Barbara from a jar she used to collect money for her yearly gambling trip and about seven hundred from Winifred that she kept in a shoe box under her bed, but she had about two thousand dollars in that box. I'm telling you...I didn't bankrupt them. I would never do that."

"So why are they lying?"

"I don't know."

"So why those two?"

She sighed. "By sheer luck I'd found a picture of Lionel on a Google search, except he didn't go under the name of Lionel Vissher. He was Lionel Proctor. I never considered that he might be living under an alias. So I started digging. That's how I found Barbara and Winifred. They worked at the library where I would use the computers. They took me in when I had nowhere to go."

"And then you stole from them?"

She stiffened. "Why do you have to say it like that?"

"Like how?"

"Like I'm some kind of vile swindler of old ladies or something."

"Cassi...I'm sorry if you don't like the facts but we need to consider all details. While you may have thought these little old ladies were sweet, it would seem they sold you out."

At that, she lost her quills. "Right," she admitted. "I'd forgotten that part." She seemed at a loss. "I don't know why they did that. I mean, I suppose anyone has a price and whoever paid them off offered them enough to make it worth their while."

"So what did you discover in Virginia?" he asked.

"Lionel Proctor was married to a wealthy woman who died unexpectedly. They'd only been married two years."

"Did you find out how she died?"

"Yeah, Winifred's daughter worked as a nurse at the hospital where Lydia Proctor died. She died of natural causes but she'd been pretty sick, just like my mom."

"Did you tell anyone?"

She shook her head. "No way. The last time I started making accusations or even pointing fingers in the direction of Lionel Vissher I lost everything. I needed to gather enough evidence to hang him, not just piss him off further. This man is dangerous. I've learned a lot in the past two years. Anyone who crosses him doesn't live to talk about it."

"He can't be that badass," Thomas said, a small smile lifting the corner of his mouth, but she just shook her head. "Okay, I see what you're saying about there being a possible similarity. I'm surprised no one else saw it and questioned him, at the very least insisted on an autopsy for your mother."

"That's just it, Lionel ingratiates himself to the people in his circles. No one believed me because... well, I'd already screwed up before that and I'd lost credibility. I think he planned it that way."

"How so?"

"Well, it's only a theory, but in the research I've done, every woman he's been connected with had two things in common—first, they were rich and second, they didn't have a lot of family or the family they did have were black sheep. My mother fit the bill perfectly."

He mulled the information around in his head. Cassi would've made a good investigator. Without resources, she'd managed to scrounge up this information using nothing more than her wits. But it'd taken its toll, he knew. He glanced back at her and he could see the fatigue pulling at her, painting dark smudges under her eyes and whittling away any extra body fat.

It was late. There was little they could do at the moment. He hadn't exactly made up his mind if he believed her but she'd created sufficient question as to whether she was guilty or not. So, for the time being, he figured it couldn't hurt to investigate things a little further. Besides, keeping her close, even under the guise of helping her, would preclude him from having to chase her all over the eastern seaboard. If the time came and he had to haul her in, after all, she was conveniently already in his possession. He could very well lose his job over this, he realized. But he was going to try to avoid that. He'd see what he could do without his supervisor knowing. He could make calls, make a few inquiries. But in the meantime, he had to make sure Cassi didn't run off again. He wasn't so naive—or at least he wasn't now after she'd made him look like a fool twice already—to think she'd stay put simply because he asked.

"Let's call it a night," he suggested as he pulled out his handcuffs. Her eyes widened and she gave him a hard stare but he had no choice. "We have a ways to go before we're BFFs, Cassi. You're in my custody until I say otherwise. I'm going to help you but until I can trust you…you're staying put."

"I promise—"

"Sorry," he cut her off, steeling himself against the plaintive look and the wounded tone in her voice. "You seem to suffer from an allergy to the truth. I can't have you run off again on some misguided attempt to fix this on your own."

"I was doing just fine until you came along and screwed everything up," she reminded him, throwing him a dark look as he clicked the cuff on her right wrist and then the other on his own. She looked at him, surprised. "How are we going to sleep like this?"

He grinned, and damn if he didn't enjoy it a little as he answered with a shrug, "Together I guess. I hope you don't snore. I'm a light sleeper."

CASSI STARED, NOT QUITE able to believe that Tommy had the balls to handcuff her after everything she'd just told him, and that he'd cuffed her to *him*.

This was wrong on so many levels. But she hadn't a choice except to allow him to curl up beside her. He kicked off his shoes but otherwise remained dressed and then tucked her into his side as if they were two spoons in a drawer. He even wrapped his arm around her middle, ostensibly for her comfort and then with his breath tickling the tiny hairs on her neck, he dropped off as if they were lazing in a cabana somewhere enjoying a siesta before dinner.

Which they certainly were not.

She held herself stiff and rigid, not wanting her backside to touch his front but that got uncomfortable quickly so when she was certain he was asleep, she allowed herself to relax, settling against the solid warmth of his chest and snuggling into the heat that emanated from his body. It wasn't long before she dropped off and slept like a rock for the first time in years.

She awoke with a start, panicked when she didn't recognize her surroundings and then groaned when her arm started to tingle from sleeping on her side all night.

Tommy rolled to his back in his sleep and she yelped when he took her arm with him. He came to with a grogginess that might've been adorable if she hadn't been in pain. "Tommy, wake up, you're killing my arm," she snapped. She'd never been a morning person even under the best of circumstances. She'd expected him to move or get up but he did neither. Instead, he picked her up and rolled her on top of him. "What are you doing?" she exclaimed, knocking him in the chest with her free hand. Then, he seemed to finally wake up and he looked chagrined to find where he'd perched her. She scooted off him and he held up his manacled hand to give her more room.

"Sorry," he mumbled, sleep roughing his voice. He scrubbed his face with his free hand and seemed to shake off the cobwebs.

Damn. Why did he have to be so handsome? He grabbed the key and unlocked the cuff from his own wrist but kept hers on. She frowned at him. He responded with a shoulder shrug. "Trust, remember? We need showers. How do you want to do this?"

She blinked, heat flooding her cheeks and other places at the thought. "What do you mean?"

"Well, if I shower that'll leave you unattended. And there's nothing in this place to handcuff you to that you couldn't bust free from. Everything here is made of flimsy wood that would shatter easily. So, I ask again...how do we accomplish basic hygiene?"

"You are not going to stand next to me while I

pee," she said, balking. "Or anything else for that matter."

He laughed. "The bathroom doesn't have any windows for you to crawl out of so I think it's okay to allow you some privacy there. The question is what do I do with you while *I* shower?"

"Maybe you'll just have to make the sacrifice and go without," she countered sweetly.

"I wouldn't be the one making the sacrifice. I'm a guy. I can go without a shower for days but I've been told the female nose is far more sensitive to those social niceties."

She made a face. Eww. He had a point. Especially if he planned to continue their sleeping arrangements the way they were last night. She lifted her chin and tried a disinterested shrug. "It's nothing I haven't seen before. If you're so worried about me escaping I guess you can handcuff me to the toilet while you shower."

She was a damn fine actress. The very thought of sitting docilely while he showered was enough to set her teeth on edge. By the way he grinned, she wondered if he saw through her bluff and enjoyed pushing her to catch her reaction. Well, two could play that game. She studied her fingernail. "Or we could just be adults about it and conserve water by showering together," she suggested.

He looked ready to bolt and she privately crowed.

Don't run with the big dogs if you're still whizzing like a puppy. She smothered a smirk as he glowered.

"That's not going to happen," he said.

She shrugged. "Whatever. Your loss."

He unlocked her cuff and she rubbed at the chafed skin as he gestured toward the bathroom. "Go do what you need to do. I have some phone calls to make," he said.

"What about you?" she asked innocently as she sauntered to the bathroom.

"I'll go without today," he muttered, and she closed the door on her own laughter.

CHAPTER NINE

THOMAS HEARD THE WATER running and Cassi humming to herself through the thin wall separating the bathroom from the bedroom and he shuddered at the thought of her, naked, water sluicing over her body, sliding over places he ached to touch and feel himself.

Last night he'd slept like a baby. Surprising, because he'd been tormented by the feel of lying so close to Cassi and unable to do anything about it. Yet, within moments his eyelids drooped and he was out like a light. It'd felt good. He couldn't remember the last time he slept so soundly.

But now, he was tormented in a different way. He wanted her so badly he was nearly obsessed with thoughts of her. He had to shake it off if he was going to find a way out of this mess for her.

Thomas grabbed the disposable cell and swore under his breath when he realized he'd forgotten to charge it and it'd died. The disposables weren't all that great for holding a charge and he should've figured that. He plugged it in and then sat at the small, wobbly table to make some notes.

Moments later he heard the door open and he refrained from turning around. With his luck she was standing there with nothing but a towel covering her. That's all he needed. He was only human for crap's sake.

"You sure you don't want to rinse off?" she asked. "I promise I won't run."

He turned and was relieved to see her dressed and actually looking sincere. He was tempted but he declined. Besides, maybe if he stank like a dog it'd keep his head where it belonged—on the case instead of on the uncomfortable fit of his jeans. Sadly that kind of logic didn't hold up. He could be marinating in his own filth and still want to get her naked.

"Thanks," he said, pulling the files together in a neat pile. "But let's just get out of here. We have some miles to cover."

"Where are we going?" she asked, a bit fearfully. He supposed trust went both ways.

"We're going to pay a visit to your old friends Barbara and Winifred."

She looked distressed as she said, "Do we have to? I can't pay them back yet."

"We have to follow the trail you were on, only this time, we've got better resources at our disposal."

"So why go back then?" she asked, almost desperately.

He sympathized, really he did, but the trail led back to those women so that's where they were going. She'd have to tough it out, no matter how unpleasant the encounter was. But he softened a little at the misery in her eyes. "Don't worry. You can stay in the car. I don't need them reporting back to whoever gave them the money that you're asking questions."

Relief flooded her gaze and for a second he thought he saw tears glittering. "Thanks," she said in a small voice. "I'm just not ready to see them yet."

"I know. But I'm not doing it only for you," he admitted. "Anything I can do to keep from losing my job for aiding and abetting a suspect is good with me."

She smiled. "Well, then I guess it's a win-win."

"In this instance…yeah, I guess it is. Grab your stuff. Let's hit the road."

CASSI FELT A MILD TWINGE of guilt for the fact that when she'd split with Tommy's car she'd also hijacked his cell phone and now he was forced to use a disposable. She supposed there was little she could do to change what had gone down so she let it be. But when she continued to feel a twinge here and there, she wondered if she was feeling more than simple guilt over the phone. He was helping her, something she hadn't expected, and he might possibly lose his job over it. She wanted to be free of this mess, but there was a possibility that nothing might come of their investigation and she didn't like the idea of Tommy going down in flames with her.

"I didn't ask you to do this," she blurted, unable to keep her thoughts private.

Tommy glanced at her before returning his gaze to the road. "I know."

"Then why are you?" she asked.

He didn't have an immediate answer. Maybe he didn't know himself. The thought wasn't a comfort. She ought to ditch him as soon as possible, if only to protect him. Of course, he wouldn't see it as such. He was all about being the big, bad protector. That strong silent thing that was ingrained in him from birth most likely, which, given his childhood, was probably a defensive mechanism.

"Cassi, I want to believe that you're innocent. Up until last night I was fairly certain you were lying, but now I know, at the very least something fishy is going on with this Lionel character. Did he commit murder? I don't know. Maybe he's just a douche and you're still a thief. But if there's a chance to prove otherwise? I can't walk away from it."

Her throat ached. It seemed a small thing, but

right now, it was huge. "Thank you," she said in a voice strangled by emotion. "It means a lot that you believe me."

"I wouldn't go that far," he muttered and her joy dimmed as the reality of the situation hit her in the face. He wasn't doing this for her, per se; he was doing it to ease his conscience. Still, beggars couldn't be choosers, she supposed, so she nodded in understanding. Her disappointment must've been evident for he softened a bit as he said, "Well, I don't like the idea of someone purposefully trying to hurt you, Cassi. If that's the case I will do everything in my power to nail him to the wall. That's a promise."

Cassi caught a glimmer of her old Tommy, the one who had once been her rock and source of strength, and her breath hitched in her throat for the bittersweet glimpse. Why hadn't she swallowed her pride and called him the minute she'd gotten into trouble? He wouldn't have turned her away, not then.

"I've been clean and sober for three years now," she revealed, the need to clear her reputation in Tommy's eyes achingly important at that moment. She needed him to know that she'd changed, that she wasn't the foolish, selfish and messed-up girl who'd kicked him out of her life so many years ago. She could still see the disgust written all over his face from their last contact.

His mouth tightened as the memory washed over him, as well. "That was a long time ago, Cassi..." he started, but she didn't want to let it go. It was important for her to get this out.

"I made a lot of mistakes. I got caught up in the lifestyle of the people I thought were my friends. I should've listened to you in the first place. They were never my friends—you were my true friend—and I wish things hadn't changed between us."

Silence filled the space between them until Tommy said, "We can't alter the past. It is what it is. You're not the same girl I used to know and you never will be. It's no one's fault...just how things turned out."

Hot tears burned behind her eyes but she nodded stiffly. "Of course. I know that. I just wanted you to know that I don't mess with drugs any longer. It felt important to mention, that's all."

He gave her a subtle incline of his head to indicate he acknowledged her but he kept any further comment to himself and Cassi was glad. She'd bared a bit of her soul to him and he'd reacted with cold indifference. It hurt more than she wanted to admit because she knew to admit it meant Tommy still owned a piece of her, even after all these years.

And that seemed pathetic given the fact that he didn't seem to want her any longer.

TOMMY FOCUSED ON THE DRIVE as they ate up the miles to Virginia but inside his head was a war zone.

Memories best left underground were clawing to the surface and he didn't seem to have control over how they behaved.

He knew she was hurt by his reaction but he couldn't help himself. Perhaps he was still angry at how she'd kicked him to the curb so easily. Maybe his wounded pride was in control at the moment and he was looking for payback. If that were the case he had nothing to be proud of, as Mama Jo would say. He glanced at Cassi and found her with her eyes shut, her head turned away from him. He couldn't walk away—so what if his reasoning was muddied? He was under no obligation to help her. He wasn't a defense attorney; it wasn't his job to ascertain guilt or innocence. Hell, he should've brought her in without getting into this mess but he'd barreled past that exit and now he had no choice but to see it through.

If he lost his job over this…he damn well deserved it.

SIX HOURS LATER THEY pulled into Virginia Beach, the salty air causing Cassi to sigh as she remembered

a few good times spent with her toes buried in the
sand, watching tourists and their families and pretending that she wasn't who she was. It was easy to
smile when you pushed away reality.

But the beach was cold and the tourists were long
gone, just like the sun for the day. It was nearing the
dinner hour and her stomach was clanging the bell
but she didn't have much cash on her so she tried to
forget about it. She always kept a water bottle in her
pack for that very purpose. You could go a long way
without food but not very far dehydrated. She took a
long swig just as Tommy pulled into a hotel parking
lot. It was nicer than the last place. A lot nicer.

"What are we doing?" she asked.

"Getting a place to stay for the night."

She glanced around. "It's a little fancy, don't you
think?"

"With tourist season over, the rooms will be
cheaper no matter where we go. So we might as
well stay someplace that doesn't smell like stale beer
and old carpet. Right?"

That made sense. Sort of. "Well, it's on your
dime. I can't afford this kind of place."

"Don't worry. I got you covered."

She gazed at the beautiful, historic hotel and
knew without a doubt that their room would have a
built-in fireplace, a four-poster bed with a sumptu-
ous goose-down comforter and sheets with a thread

count of five hundred. There was probably a mini-fridge with lots of tasty goodies and turn-down service. Back in the day, this would've been her norm. Before her life fell apart she didn't realize that hotels came below a five-star rating. Now, she knew that some hotels would have to reach to attain one star.

He turned and made quick work of taking off the cuff he'd left dangling on her wrist like an oversize bangle and said, "C'mon, let's get checked in."

For a brief moment she hesitated, contemplating for a wild, crazy, almost-desperate moment making a run for it. She didn't want to go into that beautiful hotel and remember all the things that she'd once taken for granted. But then, the pull of luxury, the idea of sinking into a king-size tub and soaking for an hour or two was too much to ignore. Good gravy...she couldn't resist.

"You coming?" he asked, eyeing her intently, watching as her internal struggle raged. She sensed his tension, knowing that he seemed to know what she was thinking and was waiting for her next move. Trust is a leap of faith, she told herself. Put one foot in front of the other and take that chance....

"Yeah..." she said. She met his stare with a tentative smile. "And try to get a room with a view. I love the ocean at night."

Time to leap...

HE MAY HAVE GONE A LITTLE overboard with the room, Thomas realized with a subtle burn in his cheeks. But the price was right, he argued with himself as he let them in.

But to call it a room was misleading. It was a suite.

The bed was a massive four-poster California King with crisp white-and-navy-blue bedding and plump pillows cascading in a decadent pile. It wasn't something he'd normally shell out a ton of coin for, but one look at Cassi's face and he knew he would've paid anything.

"Oh, it's gorgeous," she breathed. Her eyes filled with tears and she turned away so he wouldn't see, but he had. She wiped at her eyes and then turned to him, announcing in a watery voice, "I'm hungry. Let's order in."

"Good idea," he agreed, though food wasn't exactly where his head was at. He grabbed the local menus and started perusing. "What sounds good to you?"

"Whatever," she answered, moving to the sliding-glass door, where a view of the darkened seascape met the eye. She opened the door and slipped out to the small terrace. The wind kissed her face, lifting her hair and sending a draft curling through the room. He watched as she leaned into the brisk air, head tilted back, as if the air was cleansing her somehow, and he found a smile forming on his lips. Realizing he was holding the phone but hadn't ordered, he quickly dialed and placed an order for two cheeseburgers.

She returned just as he was hanging up. "How's the view?" he asked, and she smiled.

"It's amazing. You can see the white sea foam hitting the rocks but that's about it. But that's okay. I remember what it looks like. This is a beautiful place," she said, watching him with a tiny smile.

He warmed in the face of her appreciation. She was wrong…this place paled in comparison to her. But he couldn't very well admit that to her under the current circumstances. "Food should be here in about a half hour," he said brusquely, moving away so he could focus.

Sensing the change in him, she pointed to the bathroom. "I bet there's a fabulous tub in the bathroom. Mind if I check it out?"

"Be my guest," he said, but then held up a finger. "Hold on, let me check it out." She frowned in confusion but when he double-checked the exits her happiness faded a little. He was sorry for that but he had to cover his ass. "All clear. Windows are bolted. No one getting in or *out*."

She gave him a dark look as she moved past him. "Good to know," she said and then closed the door behind her.

CASSI SIGHED QUIETLY, resting her head on the door. The weight of his distrust was heavier than she imagined. Their history was both a comfort and a hindrance. She didn't want to be back in Virginia Beach and she didn't want Tommy mixed up in her mess. But even as the temptation to bolt was there, the yearning to stay was equally strong. There was something else bubbling between them besides the nostalgia of a former friendship.

It was deeper and stronger, and growing far more intense. She wanted him. And she was certain he wanted her. But to take that step would change things irrevocably between them and she was fairly certain neither of them were ready for the questions it would provoke.

Moving to the tub, she started the water and then perused the selection of bath salts offered. She selected the chamomile and white tea blend, hoping for a calming effect. Once the tub was full and the room clouded with steam, she slipped into the water with a groan of pure delight.

She couldn't remember the last time she enjoyed the simple pleasure of a bath. Most places she stayed only had showers, if she were lucky, and those with bathtubs were often caked with so much grime she bypassed them completely.

Her muscles, which had felt permanently tensed,

started to loosen and another sigh escaped her lips, only this time it was pure contentment.

She pushed away any thought that didn't involve enjoying the moment, and that included her turbulent feelings about her warden/former best friend.

THOMAS TRIED TO KEEP his thoughts on the straight and narrow. But it wasn't easy. He'd made a major error in judgment coming to a place where you'd typically bring a lover for a long weekend.

But it was as if he couldn't help himself. The places she'd been staying…her apartment, and then the hotel room…they were dives. And he could tell by the way she didn't even notice her surroundings that she'd become accustomed to living so poorly.

Cassi—born a princess and spoiled within an inch of her life living like a two-dollar hooker—it did something to him.

In school, everyone had wanted to be Cassi's friend because of her money, but she'd approached him, drawing him into her life with a pure act of kindness that you wouldn't expect from someone so accustomed to privilege.

He'd been twelve. She'd been ten and a half. He was new to the school and to his foster mother, Mama Jo. He remembered the day so clearly it hardly seemed possible that it was more than a handful of years ago.

He'd been at Asbury Park, dry-eyed but broken inside. Asbury Park was the invisible line that separated the rich from the poor. Of course, he hadn't known that, being new and all; he'd just wanted to be alone and Mama Jo had suggested he "go get some air" and "come back with a better attitude."

He didn't know what to think of the small black woman, so different from his own mother, who'd been buried along the rest of his family, and he was pretty lost in his new surroundings.

Cassie had appeared, wearing a pretty pink dress with a brand-new camera slung around her neck and her hair in springy, white curls. Her features were fine-boned and delicate; even as a young girl she'd been quite beautiful, though at that time he hadn't been looking for anything aside from solitude.

He hadn't invited her to sit with him. In fact, he may have scowled and told her to go away—he couldn't remember. But she seemed to see beyond his prickly exterior as she sat next to him, chatting away.

That's how it'd started. One act of kindness.

He sighed. He might've fallen in love with her that day. Too bad he never had the balls to tell her.

Not even after they'd kissed. And certainly not after he watched guy after guy come into her life and he'd remained on the sidelines as the friend and confidant.

And now she was in the other room, naked and wet.

He shook his head and shoved to his feet a bit too quickly when the soft knock at the door signaled the food had arrived.

He paid the deliveryman and gave him a good tip. He hadn't been all that hungry but the smell was reviving his appetite. "Grub's on," he called out, knowing Cassi would appear quickly. She'd always been a slave to her stomach, which is why he'd been surprised to see how thin she'd become.

The sound of the water draining brought a smile to his lips. A minute later she appeared, hair piled in a messy bun on her head, folded into a thick, white terry cloth robe, courtesy of the hotel.

He glanced down at his burger and then back to her. She looked good enough to eat herself. "Don't let it get cold," he advised, right before taking a huge bite of his burger.

She took a seat on the small love seat beside him and, tucking her feet under her, she lifted her burger and took a healthy bite. "Good stuff," she murmured, savoring it. "Been a long time since I've had decent food."

"I'll bet," he said around the bite in his mouth. He wiped up with a napkin before saying, "I remembered that you don't like onions."

She nodded with a brief smile full of gratitude. "It's perfect," she said.

"So I'm curious…" he said between bites. "When you came up with your false identity in New York you made Trinity Moon a vegan. I happen to know for a fact that you love meat."

"Yeah, exactly," she said, her cheeks full. She chewed and swallowed, grinning. "I try to make my identities as real as possible—that way I don't slip up. Trinity didn't believe in eating anything with a face. At first it was hard to give up meat but after a while I stopped craving it. I did get very pale, though."

He laughed. "That's quite a sacrifice for your identity."

"Hey, pretending to be someone you're not is serious business. It's like an acting job but there's no director wrapping the set after a long day."

He sobered. "I guess." Then he said, "Maybe when this is all over you could go to Hollywood, get an acting job, seeing as you've had all this experience pretending to be someone else."

"No, thanks. When this is all over, I don't want to be anyone but myself for a change."

He grinned and took another bite of his burger. He liked the sound of that.

CHAPTER TEN

LATER, WHILE CASSI FLIPPED through the channels and Thomas spent some time on the phone with a peer, she watched him covertly. He'd matured into such a handsome man. She hadn't seen a ring on his finger, not that that meant he was single. He could very well have a girlfriend somewhere. The thought gave her an uncomfortable twinge. She returned to the television but her interest was far from anything circulating on the networks. She gave up and shut it off.

"Tired?" he asked, looking up from his notes.

"No."

"What's wrong?"

"Bored."

He chuckled, then gestured to his paperwork strewn about the table. "We could talk shop."

She wrinkled her nose. "I'd rather not. Seems a travesty to waste an amazing room on work. Tomorrow will come soon enough," she muttered, not looking forward to what was on the agenda. "Come talk with me."

He lost his smile and seemed wary. "I don't think that's a good idea," he said.

"Why?"

He sighed and shook his head. "It's just not."

Cassi cocked her head and watched him for a moment. A little furrow in his brow told her he was trying really hard to focus. He used to get that same look when he was studying algebra. He'd never really had a head for abstract concepts. But as Cassi had said then, and it certainly had played out true enough—who mixes letters and numbers in real life anyway?

"Do you have a girlfriend?" she asked suddenly.

Her question startled him and it took a minute for him to recover. When he did, he simply shook his head.

"Why not?"

He shrugged. "Just haven't found someone who wanted to put up with my schedule I guess."

"You work long hours?"

"Long hours, weekends, holidays…"

"Oh. Do you have to work that kind of schedule or do you choose to? There's a difference, you know."

He met her gaze. "I choose to."

"Maybe if you had someone you wanted to spend time with you'd want to spend less time at work."

"It's a theory," he agreed mildly. "But since I

haven't found that person yet…it's a moot point. Besides, I love my job."

"Does the job love you back?"

He chuckled again, shaking his head. "She's a tough mistress."

She moved from the sofa and over to where he was sitting. He watched her approach with a smile that seemed to hide something else beneath it. She smiled and held out her hand to him. "I remember someone having magic hands. Come give me a back massage for old time's sake."

"I don't know, Cassi," he said, and she detected a subtle strain to his voice.

She ignored his mild protest and pulled him from the chair. "C'mon, there's no harm in giving a girl a massage. Besides, it's been a long time since I've had anyone with your skill and if all this goes south and I end up going to prison, at least I'll have a few good memories."

"Don't talk like that," he said, clearly uncomfortable with the idea of her going to prison. "We don't know how this is going to play out, yet."

"That's the hope but let's be realistic. Or on second thought, let's not be realistic for the moment. Just rub," she said, climbing on the bed and flopping on her stomach. She wiggled out of the robe and shimmied it down to her waist while still managing to keep her private parts covered modestly. She felt the bed give under his weight and she smothered a triumphant grin. She heard him exhale a shaky breath and she knew without a doubt she was going to enjoy every moment, no matter what it cost her.

THE MINUTE THOMAS PUT HIS hands on Cassi's smooth skin, he knew he'd just stepped over the threshold of hell. He should've said no. He should've gone for a walk and gotten some fresh air to clear his head. But the minute she shrugged out of her robe, his feet had been on autopilot and he'd been drawn as surely as a bee unerringly finds the pollen.

Back when they were kids he would coax the knots from her shoulders and she would help him with his homework. That was the exchange. She said no one had the magic touch like he did. Not even the fancy Swedish masseurs who came to her house for her parents. He wasn't sure he believed that but he'd been flattered nonetheless, and any excuse to touch her was fine with him.

Her skin felt like silk beneath his fingertips. Her spine was a delicate line of bone that spread to the gentle flare of her hips. He could see the plump sides of her breasts while she lay on her stomach. She was quite honestly the most perfect female specimen on the planet as far as he was concerned.

"Tommy…do you ever think of your dad?" she asked, her tone solemn.

"I try not to," he answered truthfully.

"Do you ever visit your mom's and brother's graves?"

"No," he admitted. He couldn't bring himself to, even after all these years. Some nights he could still hear his mother's screams and see his little brother's terrified stare. "Going to their graves isn't going to bring them back."

"Yeah. I know. I didn't visit my dad's grave, either. I mean, I know it's not the same. My dad wasn't like yours but...I never wanted to go to that damn cemetery. My mom was always pushing it on me, though. Like I didn't love him if I didn't go and sit by a stone with his name on it."

He remained silent, choosing to concentrate on her shoulders instead. But she'd awakened bad memories and now they were running through his head.

"I always wondered how you ended up in Mama Jo's care," she said wistfully. "I mean, I always thought it was odd that you, Christian and Owen— three white kids—ended up with a single black woman."

He shrugged. "Mama Jo had a reputation within the social services of having a way with the problem kids. Given our backgrounds, they probably figured they'd skip a step and just stick us with Mama Jo first and see what happened."

"She's one helluva woman," Cassi said.

"That she is," he agreed.

"So what would she say if she knew what you were doing?"

"Rubbing your back?" he asked.

"You know what I mean," she returned softly, and he supposed he did but it was a loaded question. Mama Jo was very proud that he'd gone into law enforcement, and she'd been disappointed to hear how things had ended between him and Cassi but he doubted she'd embrace this craziness he was participating in right now. Likely, if he told her, she'd just scold him for being reckless and then stuff him full of corn bread. He stilled, and Cassi turned to face him, clutching the robe to her chest. She met his gaze and a tiny smile lifted the corner of his mouth as his body temperature rose in time with the pulsing heat from his groin. "She always liked you," he answered, moving toward her. "Said you were made of tougher stuff than anyone realized, including yourself, and someday you'd figure that out."

A look of surprise crossed her features. "Wow. She said that about me?"

"Yeah…" he murmured, his eyes feasting on the creamy flesh that was exposed. He ought to get off the bed and put his mind back on work but he couldn't. It would've taken a Herculean effort, and frankly, at the moment, he felt weak as a newborn colt, shaking out his legs for the first time. "Cassi," he whispered. The effort it took not to kiss her was taking everything he had and he didn't know how much longer he could hold out.

"What is it, Tommy?" she asked, sounding a bit breathless herself.

"If you don't get off this bed right now…I'm going to kiss you and I probably won't want to stop there," he said with blunt honesty. "If that's not what you want then you better say something right now."

She swallowed, her gaze going wide and then she said in a husky whisper, "I'm not saying a word…"

Sweet heaven, if he was going to lose everything, this might very well make it worth it.

TOMMY DIDN'T WAIT. Maybe he was afraid she'd change her mind, but if he knew what was traveling through her thoughts he'd know better. She wanted him so badly yet hadn't known how to make a move that didn't come off feeling desperate or manipulative. The back rub excuse hadn't been her most inventive, but it'd worked even if it'd never worked in high school.

Tommy's lips touched hers and she swore her heart stopped from the sheer electricity arcing between them. His touch was firm and hungry and when his tongue tangled with hers, she nearly tore off his clothes in her urgency to feel more. Within minutes her robe slid from her body and she reveled in the rasp of his mouth against the sensitive skin of her neck and then lower to her breasts. She drew a wild breath as he sucked one nipple into his mouth while his searching hand found her other breast and squeezed gently. She arched into his mouth and he obliged by sucking hard, sending a dark thrill straight down to her toes.

She grabbed a fistful of his hair and held him at her breast, urging him to devour her. He sucked, laved and teased her nipples until she couldn't stand another minute of the sensual torture. It was good and it'd been so long since she'd been touched by anyone. But it wasn't just that and she knew it. It was Tommy. Her heart sang as loudly as her body as his fingers and tongue plundered her most secret spots, causing her to twist handfuls of the soft duvet between her fists, drawing a cry from her lips even as her body quivered from pent-up need and frustrated desire. So many years of being close to him yet not being able to touch because she hadn't wanted to ruin the precious and fragile nature of their relationship. His friendship had grounded her, kept her from spinning off and losing herself in the shallow pools of her most conceited and self-absorbed circles. He'd been her touchstone, and oh, God, how she'd missed him!

THOMAS COULD BARELY CONTAIN himself, struggling to hold his desire in check so that he could wring every last whimper of pleasure from Cassi's body. He wanted to show her with his actions how much he'd always loved her, how he'd been adrift in a sea of faces for years until that file crossed his desk. He hadn't walked away for a reason and he was feeling it now.

Her breathy moans excited and teased him to the point where it took all he had to keep from plunging into her body with abandon. But he wouldn't do that. Not with Cassi…he would draw out every moan until neither could stand another minute without reaching completion.

She shuddered beneath him, the taste of her still on his tongue, and when she was limp and trying to catch her breath, he flipped her to her stomach. While he could've taken forever to admire the smooth, sweet curve of her ass, he needed to feel her close around him with an urgency that stunned him.

She lifted her hips in invitation and he gladly took it, sliding into the promised land with a guttural moan. She gasped as he seated himself, heavy and thick, into her sheath and it was all he could do not to shout his pleasure as his eyes rolled into the back of his head. He started slow, rubbing against the elusive spot with the tip of his erection and delighted in the way she twisted and arched against him. But soon, it was all he could take and his hips pushed forward, urging him to go faster and harder. She gasped but met him thrust for thrust, greedy for every inch he could give, and when she let out a strangled cry he let go and gave in to the bone-rattling orgasm that clenched every muscle so hard he thought he might cramp. He collapsed against her, the scent of her hair deep in his nostrils and when he could string together a coherent thought he was sunk by the realization that he'd do anything for this woman...even if it meant breaking the law.

And that scared the hell out of him.

CHAPTER ELEVEN

THE NEXT MORNING CASSI awoke half sprawled across Tommy, one leg over his and her head resting nicely on his chest. She stretched, nuzzling the tight muscle of his chest and inhaling the scent of his skin mingled with that of their lovemaking. This was, she thought muzzily, the nicest way to wake up. Her hand drifted down his stomach, searching and finding what she wanted. His sharp intake of breath made her smile as her hand tightened on the silken shaft, hard and ready, throbbing in her hand.

So when he gently removed her hand, she was understandably confused. She sat up and looked down at him. "What's wrong?" she asked.

"Nothing," he answered, but his eyes told a different story.

"Oh, my God...was this like a...booty call?" she asked, horrified at the very thought, given how she'd entered into it with a totally different mind-set. As in, "Holy shit I think I love this man" when he was acting as if he was thinking, "Can't wait to tap that and then skip out before she wakes up."

His brow wrinkled in obvious distaste at the term *booty call* and she lost some of her tension but none of her confusion. He smoothed the hair from her face with such tenderness that she could only stare. "You're giving me some really mixed signals, Tommy. Your hands say that you want me but your eyes are saying keep your distance. What's going on?"

He sighed and sat up, a bleak expression haunting his eyes. He scrubbed his hands over his face as if trying to wipe away whatever was bothering him and when he looked at her again, it seemed as if he'd succeeded, which she found suspicious. When he answered, it was with no indication of his previous thoughts. "I do want you. But I need to focus," he said sternly. "There's a lot at stake here, Cassi. Not just for you. But for me, too. I don't want to lose my job and I don't want you to go to prison. As much as I'd like to stay in this bed and make love to you all day, that's not going to solve the problem. We need to talk with Barbara and Winifred and see what we can uncover about their mystery benefactor. Hopefully, they'll give us something to go from. If not, we'll move to your friend Isaac."

At the mention of Isaac she winced. "Do we have to?"

"Unfortunately, yes. Trust me, I'd rather skip that one, too."

She cast a sidewise glance. "I know why I don't want to see him… Why don't you want to see him?"

He leaned forward and surprised her with a firm, possessive kiss on her lips before saying, "Because for years I watched other guys kiss these lips and I hated them for it. To know this guy actually proposed…makes me want to put my fist through his face."

Her cheeks flushed and her heartbeat fluttered like a schoolgirl's at the sight of her first crush. She managed a small coy smile as she said, "Well…I can't help that someone else beat you to it."

At that he stilled, and she realized she'd said something wrong though for the life of her she didn't know what it could be. She faltered. "I didn't mean anything by that," she said, frowning in embarrassment. "I was just kidding. Of course, I never expected you to propose to me or anything…."

He looked away, and she sensed his disquiet had less to do with her and more to do with himself but it hurt just the same. She withdrew and he caught her hand. "Cassi," he said quietly. "All things being perfect, if there were ever a woman I'd even contemplate marrying…you'd be it. But the fact is, I lied when I said no one was willing to put up with my schedule and that's why I was unattached."

A cold knot had begun to form and she didn't

want to hear the rest. "Forget it, Tommy. Whatever it is, I don't need to know."

"No, I need to tell you this because you're probably the only person who'd ever understand." That piqued her interest and she peered at him with open concern. He continued, and that bleak expression returned. "I never want to marry anyone."

"Why, Tommy?"

"Do you even have to ask? Because marriage messes with people's heads and makes them do crazy things. It's that whole death-do-us-part thing that's just wrong. I mean, what if people change and then your partner doesn't like the person you've become? And then they do terrible things to each other in the name of love? No...I'm not willing to take that on. I'm just not."

Realization hit her and she actually felt tears welling in her eyes. She wanted to reach out to him but didn't touch him. She didn't trust herself not to wrap him in a huge hug and she sensed that he needed a little distance. "You know all marriages aren't like your parents'," she said softly. "Not all husbands do what your father did."

She knew that logically Tommy understood this but there was something deep inside, locked away in a private place, that kept an irrational fear alive and rabid.

"You know, he didn't start out bad. He loved my

mother so much it drove him crazy, twisted him up inside until he didn't know what was right or wrong anymore. That's the danger of that kind of love."

She shook her head. "No, that's not love. That's… a perversion of love. Love doesn't try to subvert another's will or possess. True love is giving and kind."

"How do you know?" he asked, his mouth twisting. "Your parents didn't have a model marriage, either. Your father had his share of extracurricular activities and your mother was perpetually unhappy."

She drew back, mildly hurt by his mocking tone and the fact that he was using information from her past as ammunition against her. "There's no such thing as a model marriage. You're smart enough to know that. If you're going to push me away, have the guts to admit the true reasons you're doing it. Push me away because I'm on the run from the law and you don't want the complication, or push me away because all you truly wanted was a booty call. But don't let fear of something that isn't true keep you from being happy." She leaned forward and tenderly cupped his face with both hands as she made her final point. "You are not your father. And you never could be, Thomas Eric Bristol. I know this in my heart and nothing you say will ever change that. Got it? Marry, don't marry…I don't care but don't let your father take even more from you than he already did." She pressed a kiss to his mouth before he could say anything else. And then she scrambled from the bed, announcing, "I'm going to shower. You're welcome to join me if you like."

Without waiting for his answer, she strode, naked as a jaybird, to the bathroom.

THOMAS STARED AFTER HER and he realized he was shaking. He hadn't meant to say those things but they just fell out of his mouth. Now he wished he could reel them back. It was a knee-jerk reaction to her teasing, and he'd just made himself look like a complete ass without provocation. He bounced his head against the headboard with a growl at himself. *Way to go, Ace.*

He climbed out of the bed and went to salvage whatever was happening between them before he destroyed the first chance he'd ever had at satisfying the ache in his heart since the day they'd parted ways.

He didn't know where this was going—he didn't dare think beyond the next twenty-four hours—but he knew that he'd unleashed something that wouldn't return to its cage nicely. He could already feel the scratches across his heart and he knew with certainty that before this was done, he'd be lucky to walk away at all.

They pulled up to trailer space No. 15 in the Dogwood Acres trailer park. Since Cassi had dyed her hair and had donned a low-brimmed hat to wait in the car, he figured neither lady would recognize their sticky-fingered friend.

He walked up the three steps to the door and took careful note of his surroundings. Barbara Hanks wasn't living large, that was for sure. The trailer was of the ancient variety, though the stairs looked fairly new in comparison. He gave the door a knock and waited.

The overcast sky mirrored the turbulent waves that he could hear rolling into the shore, and it was cold enough to warrant a jacket. He glanced around, looking for signs of life, and when a second knock elicited no answer, he walked the perimeter. In the back, he found a woman sweeping the walking stones that led to a withered garden.

"Hello?" he called out, causing the older lady to squint at him in wary confusion. He flashed his badge. "Do you know where I can find Barbara Hanks?"

"This here is her place," the woman answered with a strong Virginian accent, still eyeing him with faint suspicion. "What you want Barb for?"

"Just looking to ask her some questions," he said mildly. "Do you know where I can find her?"

She pursed her lips and returned to sweeping.

"She can't answer your questions. She done passed last night. Bless her soul, she's gone to Jesus. I was just cleaning up a bit before they come to get her things."

It could be coincidence that Barbara Hanks kicked the bucket soon after receiving a nice payout from someone for filing a false report against Cassi. Then again...in his line of work, coincidences were few and far between.

"You're a friend of Ms. Hanks?" he asked.

"Best and only friend," she said, lifting her chin. "My trailer is just two spaces down."

"Are you Winifred Jones?" he surmised, and she nodded, a crinkle in her brow.

"How'd you know my name? What's going on here, lawman?"

"I'm investigating a case that you might be familiar with from a few years back...Lydia Proctor... name ring a bell at all?"

She thought for a minute then nodded slowly. "I might've seen the name somewhere, can't recall where, though. Why?"

"Lydia may have been poisoned by her husband," he answered, watching for her reaction. If his suspicion was right and the money in Winifred's account was also a payout, then it might serve to reason that Winifred wasn't safe, either. He needed to know how much she knew about her benefactor and if anything she knew could lead him back to Lionel Vissher. "Winifred, I'm going to cut to the chase. A few days ago there was a significant deposit into your account. Mind if you tell me where it came from?"

"I reckon that's my business, son," she answered coolly but her eyes registered nervousness. "I think it's getting too cold for these old bones. Good luck with your case."

"If my hunch is correct, you and your friend were offered a considerable amount of money to make false charges against someone you both knew. And now your friend is dead. Don't you find it interesting that a few days after the check clears, your friend dies? If I were you I'd be worried that someone is cleaning up loose ends."

She stopped, fidgeting with the broom handle, her thin lips pursing with consternation…or was it fear? Then she shook her head and shooed him away. "Barb died of natural causes. And I don't know what you're talking about."

"Winnie."

Cassi's voice bringing up the rear made him curse under his breath. When she was by his side he muttered, "You were supposed to stay in the car."

She ignored him and went to the old lady. Winifred's eyes reflected something that looked a lot like shame, and she almost couldn't meet Cassi's gaze. That said a lot in his book. The woman was guilty, which he figured anyway, but she felt bad about it and that was going to work in their favor.

"Winnie...what happened when I left?" she asked softly.

Winifred looked away, her mouth buttoning up as if she had no intention of answering but then she exhaled slowly and gestured for them to follow her. "Come on, it's too cold to stand out here and freeze. I'll make some coffee and we'll talk." She turned to give Cassi a short look. "And you, missy, owe me an explanation, too."

"I know," she said simply and that was enough for the old woman. She nodded and showed them the way to her trailer, which, aside from the bleached plastic flowers, was nearly identical to Barb's.

He watched as Cassi helped Winnie up the short stairs, her touch gentle and sure in spite of the fact that this woman had helped set bad things in motion for her, and he was struck by her innate kindness. That was Cassi to her core. He should've questioned the facts in the investigation from the beginning but he hadn't been willing to open that door for fear of what he might find.

Well, it was too late to stop now. And he didn't want to, either.

CHAPTER TWELVE

CASSI HELPED WINNIE INTO her favorite recliner and then grabbed the throw blanket draped along the faded sofa to tuck around her. "Why were you out in the cold, Winnie?" she asked. "That's not good for you. You'll catch pneumonia again and who will take care of you?"

Winifred waved away Cassi's concern but accepted the ministrations, her gaze taking in all the changes in Cassi's appearance as she and Tommy took a seat on the sofa.

"The brown doesn't suit you, you know," she announced critically. "Too harsh for your fair skin tone. Washes you out."

"Well, complementary wasn't what I'd been going for. I just needed a change and I needed it quick. Seems someone told the police I'd stolen a bit of money from them," she chided Winifred lightly, and the older woman lifted her chin.

"Well, you did," Winnie said.

"True. But not as much as you said. And I'm in a lot of trouble because of what you and Barb told the police. Tell me what's going on. I don't understand why you did that. I was going to pay you back as soon as I got things figured out. And you know I would never empty your bank account like you said I did. Winnie…I cared for you."

"But you stole from me. Used me for my money."

"Be realistic. You're not exactly living high on the hog. I only took enough to get me to my next destination. And look." She pulled her date book from her pack and flipped it to the page where she'd written every person's name to whom she owed something. "See?" She pointed to Winifred's name and the amount she took. "I wasn't going to forget."

Winifred grabbed her reading glasses and peered at the ledger. She swallowed and removed her glasses, her expression dimmed and her shoulders bowed. "I was so hurt. Why didn't you just ask for the money? I'd have given it to you."

"If I'd have asked I would've had to explain how I wasn't who I said I was. My stepfather is a dangerous man. He killed my mother. I've been searching for a way to prove it and he's been trying to silence me since the day he had me arrested in my family's home for assault. My name is Cassandra Nolan. I come from a very wealthy family but my stepfather has control of the family fortune since my mother's death. He's a very bad man and I think he's been killing women for a very long time. Remember when

I had your daughter look into the death of Lydia Proctor? That was one of his wives. I think he killed her, too."

"That's where I knew the name," Winifred exclaimed softly. "I was going plum crazy trying to remember."

"Lionel is trying to get me put away so he can have full control of the money without anyone getting in the way. Winnie...who paid you to lie to the cops?"

Winifred looked away but didn't answer right away. When she did, it was with a slight tremble. "It seemed a small thing...I was so hurt you'd stolen from me. A man came to me and said that if I made out like you stole a lot more than you'd taken he'd give me thirty thousand dollars. Same with Barb. He said no one would find out and he'd take care of everything. That you were a bad person and this would help bring you to justice. I don't know what I was thinking. I should've known better. But, I was behind on my taxes and was about to lose my trailer.... I thought it was a small thing, seeing as how you were a criminal and all."

"It's okay. You couldn't have known. I did lie about who I was and I did take money from you. I don't blame you for thinking the worst of me but you put yourself in danger not only from whoever offered you the bribe but from the law, too."

"I don't want to go to prison," Winnie said fearfully. "I just didn't want to lose my trailer. It's all I've got in the world anymore. Susie is busy with her own life and her husband is a bear of a man, besides. I couldn't imagine being nowhere but in my own bed, in my own house."

"It's okay, Winnie," Cassi murmured, sharing a look with Tommy. "Tell me about the man who offered you the money."

"Well, he was nice enough. Seemed real sincere. I didn't catch his name." She frowned, trying to remember. Suddenly her face lit up with something and she gestured for Cassi to grab her purse from the kitchen counter. Cassi did as she asked and Winnie rummaged around until she found what she was looking for. She exclaimed, holding a card. "Here it is. He gave me a business card. Told me to call if you came around again."

Cassi took the card and then handed it to Tommy as she said, "I don't recognize the name but I'm sure I've only scratched the surface of the lives Lionel Vissher has lived."

"How would Lionel know to look for you here?" Tommy asked, thinking out loud.

Cassi winced. "Well, I sort of sent him a message when I was here."

"What?" Tommy did a double take. "Why would you do that?"

"I wanted him to be afraid," Cassi answered, feeling sheepish. "I mean, I wanted him to know that I'd uncovered one of his deep, dark secrets and I was going to expose him. In hindsight, it doesn't seem very smart."

"At least you said it so I didn't have to," Tommy grumbled. "Anything else you might like to share?"

"Okay, I'll give you it was dumb on my part but you don't have to rub it in," Cassi retorted, looking away from Tommy. Like he never made mistakes. Yeah, right. She returned to Winifred. "So, tell me how Barb died. You said it was natural causes…how do you know?"

"Oh, she got real sick, honey. I know you're chasing after a bad man but it seems unlikely he did her in. She came down with some nasty bug…throwing up and whatnot. The doctors, they weren't sure what went wrong."

Cassi felt a chill. "Did they check for poison?"

Winifred looked aghast. "Poison? Whatever for? You don't think…" She paled. "Oh, heavens. That's a terrible thought."

Cassi got to her feet and went to the small kitchen. "Have you received anything lately? Candies? Or chocolates? Anything in the mail?"

Winifred took a minute to think it over and then she nodded slowly. "Come to think of it, I got a package of fruit bars but they had nuts so I didn't eat them." She leaned toward Cassi and said as if it were a secret, "I'm terribly allergic you know. They're over there on top of the Frigidaire. I was going to give them to Susie. That husband of hers is like a garbage disposal. The man will eat anything reasonably seasoned or sweet."

Tommy was up before Cassi said anything. He found the box and, grabbing a big, yellow latex glove from the kitchen sink, he opened it carefully. "Did this come sealed?" he asked.

"Well, sure it was," Winifred said, frowning. "Why?"

Tommy examined the box gingerly, careful to touch it as little as possible. He peered at the carton. "Yeah, this was tampered with. There are two seals here. The first one is taped over to make it look like it wasn't touched. I'm willing to bet my pension that there's a nasty surprise waiting for you in this box."

Winifred swallowed and her hand fluttered to her chest. "Oh, dear," she said, watching as Tommy found a plastic bag and put the contaminated box inside. "Why would someone want to hurt me? I've never done anyone any harm. Been a good, taxpaying citizen my whole life. Why?"

Cassi's answer was grim. "You're a loose end. I'm sorry, Winnie, for getting you mixed up with this.

You're not safe here. Can you stay with Susie for a few days until we get things figured out?"

Winifred nodded but didn't look too happy about it. "Susie's husband isn't going to like it and I won't much neither but I don't much like the idea of dying so I guess I'll go pack an overnight bag."

"Sounds good," Cassi said, helping Winifred from her chair as she shambled to the back bedroom. Cassi turned to Tommy. "Do you have any friends who can analyze these things?"

"Yeah. But I can't continue to stay off radar with that kind of request."

Cassi nodded, understanding what he was really saying. She could put her trust in him and go with him to the authorities and possibly clear her name as well as put Lionel away where he belonged—assuming anyone believed her—or she could continue to skulk in the shadows, alone and afraid, with little hope of finding justice for anyone. Well, when she laid it out like that it didn't seem like much of a choice. She exhaled a deep, heavy breath and prayed she wasn't making a huge mistake. "Make the call," she told Tommy. "Time to see just how big an influence Lionel has in the circles that count."

"It's going to be all right," Tommy assured her, but somehow she felt as if she'd just signed her own death warrant. Hopefully, she was wrong.

THEY RETURNED TO THE HOTEL room with the plan to drive to Pittsburgh the following day so that Cassi could turn herself in and Thomas could help exonerate her.

The old lady had been safely deposited with her none-too-happy son-in-law, and Cassi seemed marginally relieved that her friend was secure for the night but she was still on edge and he knew why. He couldn't blame her.

Two years on the run with no contact with family or friends was hard on a person.

When Thomas exited the shower, he found her curled in a chair beside the window, staring out at the darkened water.

He went to her and threaded his fingers through her hair. Her eyelids fluttered closed on a breath but he could feel the tension coiling in her body.

"It's going to be okay," he promised. "With the new information the charges will be dropped and we can get on with the business of actually catching this guy."

"I just can't shake this feeling that there's something else waiting in the wings, some other nasty surprise, like what was waiting for Winnie in that fruit bar box."

He understood her fear. She'd become conditioned to trust no one. It was natural that she'd mistrust the idea of going home without the force of an armed escort.

"Tell me what you know about Lionel," he suggested, if only to keep her mind occupied. She was skittish, and while he wanted to believe that she'd given up her deceptive ways, skittish people did desperate things when they felt cornered. He'd already seen that firsthand with Cassi.

She shook her head and waved away his suggestion. "I've already told you most of it. The fact is, two years worth of my life searching for clues resulted in very little real evidence. Mostly, I was just trying to stay alive and out of jail. I only found two names, Lydia Proctor and Sylvia Williams, aside from his first wife, Penelope Hogue, who died from cancer. She's the only one I think he didn't kill."

"What did you find out about Penelope?"

She shrugged. "Not much. She was also the only one who didn't come with a sizable bank account. He did get a life insurance payout, though."

"How'd you get that information?"

Her cheeks pinked. "Isaac. He worked for the same insurance company where Lionel and Penelope held the policy. It was also the only marriage where Lionel used his real name."

"Maybe he loved her." Cassi made a sour face and he lifted his hands. "It's possible. What did you learn about them through Isaac?"

She shifted, clearly uncomfortable with the conversation, but she answered, "Actually, Isaac knew Penelope pretty well. They were shirttail relatives or something. Isaac said Lionel was heartbroken when Penelope died and that the payout was only about $250,000. Not a lot of money when it was all said and done. Isaac also said Lionel left town shortly after she died, saying he couldn't bear to be surrounded by all the memories."

"Isaac never suspected any foul play?"

"No. In fact, he spoke pretty highly of the guy."

"So what led you to New York?" he asked, trying to connect the dots of her travels.

She sighed. "One of the things I found from Isaac after meeting with his family for the engagement party was that Lionel had family in upstate New York. I was following a lead. All I knew was that the Visshers were upscale socialites but Isaac said that side of the family didn't have much to do with Lionel's. Some kind of family feud."

"What were you trying to find?"

She lifted her shoulders in a helpless shrug, fatigue showing. "I don't know. Just something I could use to link him to the other women."

He hated to see her looking so lost and worried. It was a side of Cassi he'd never seen when they were kids. She'd been fearless and even reckless in her disregard for rules, discipline or anything that didn't subscribe to her individual brand of independence. She'd had the charisma of a superstar and hadn't been afraid to use it. He smiled and her brow furrowed.

"What's so funny?" she asked, pushing her hand through her hair in an agitated motion. "My friend is dead, and we're no closer to proving anything about Lionel and yet, I'm about to turn myself over to the mercy of the FBI, which coincidentally, hasn't been known to have a soft side, so I'm not seeing anything worth grinning about."

He leaned forward and pressed his lips to hers, silencing her. When he pulled away, she met his gaze and held it. "I'm scared, Tommy," she whispered.

"I won't let anything happen to you," he promised, gently pulling her from the chair, leading her to the bed. "Come lie down. You look exhausted."

"Thanks," she said wryly but she climbed onto the bed nonetheless, her mouth twitching with a smile as he followed. "What's on your mind?" she asked, leaning back against the numerous pillows plumped against the headboard.

"You."

A shiver cascaded down her body and he wanted to follow it with his tongue. He climbed her lean form until he was right above her, looking down into that beautiful face as she smiled. "And what do you plan to do with me?"

Pounding need rushed his shaft and all thoughts of the case fled his mind. All he could think of was Cassi and how little time they had before everything got very real. He didn't know how things were going to end when they got to the field office in Pittsburgh. He felt fairly certain it would go their way but there were too many variables he couldn't control. His job had been to bring her back. And he hadn't forgotten that. For now, he had her in his arms and that was what he was focusing on. Tomorrow would bring its own troubles. Tonight was all about pleasure. He gathered her tight and growled against her mouth right before taking it, "Everything."

CHAPTER THIRTEEN

THOMAS WENT THROUGH security with Cassi behind him and felt eyes on him as he passed through the Bureau office in Pittsburgh. They'd gotten up early and driven straight through, making good time on the seven-hour drive from Virginia Beach. The ride was mostly silent but Cassi had bitten her nails down to the quick.

Thomas went straight to the director and closed the door behind them.

Director George Zell eyed Thomas and then Cassi before asking, "Mind introducing me to your friend?"

"This is Cassi Nolan."

Zell sat a little straighter, his gaze darting from Cassi to Thomas and then back to Cassi again. "Any reason she's not in cuffs, Agent Bristol?"

"We have new evidence in the case, sir. Barbara Hanks is dead and Winifred Jones has recanted her statement. We also have reason to believe someone tried to kill Jones to keep her quiet after she took money to issue a false statement against Ms. Nolan."

Zell, a hard man with a shock of white hair on his Charlie Brown head, pursed his lips at the revelation. "Your job was to bring her in. You've succeeded. Now take her to booking."

Thomas felt rather than saw Cassi's alarm and rising panic. "Sir, I think there's more to this case than we originally thought," he began, but Zell cut him off.

"That will be all, Agent Bristol. Take her to booking and then report back to me when you're through."

Cassi's eyes widened and she gave a minute shake of her head and he knew she was going to bolt. "She's innocent," he protested but two agents appeared and grabbed her arms. She shrieked and started kicking and Thomas felt the situation sliding out of his control. He moved to his superior's desk and slammed the surface with his hand. "Listen to me, damn it. She's innocent! The man who sent the Bureau after her is a killer. He's used multiple aliases to prey on rich women. I'll show you!"

Zell motioned to the agents and they dragged Cassi away even as she twisted and jerked trying to get free. Thomas moved to follow but Zell's voice commanding him to stay put stopped him. He bit back the swear words filling his mouth. He was this close to tanking his career and for what? He couldn't very well bust her out of lockup. His best bet to help her would be to stay calm. He knew this intellectually but right now he was tempted to say "Screw it" and charge after the agents muscling Cassi from the room. He turned to Zell and he knew his eyes were hot. "What the hell is going on?" he demanded.

"Sit down, Bristol," Zell commanded. "You're losing your head over this woman. Your assignment was to bring her in. Job done. Now move on."

Thomas pressed his lips together in an effort to stay calm but his heart rate was erratic and all he could think of was that Cassi was probably thinking he betrayed her. "Sir, I have information—"

"So do I," Zell interrupted. He tossed a file at him. "We have new information on your friend." Thomas grabbed the file and opened it while Zell kept talking. "Before we go any further, I knew you and Nolan had history. I figured it would work to our advantage in bringing her in. Seems I wasn't wrong. But what you probably don't know is that your friend—the one proclaiming to be innocent— is wanted for murder. The theft charges were a bonus."

"What?" he said in a breath, his chest hurting as if someone had thrown a sledgehammer into his ribs. "What are you talking about?" But Zell didn't need to answer. Thomas could read it in black-and-white. Cassi was wanted for murdering her mother.

"No." He shook his head. "This is wrong. Where'd you get this?"

"A good source," he answered, but Thomas wasn't ready to let it go.

"This is still my case and I want to know where this new information is coming from. If it's from Lionel Vissher, the information is no good. The man is a possible sociopath and it serves his purpose to have Cassi out of the way."

"What are you talking about?" Zell demanded. "Lionel Vissher has been nothing but cooperative with this investigation in spite of the personal embarrassment of having a criminal for a stepdaughter."

Thomas looked at Zell. Something about his statement sounded off-key to him. "You tight with Vissher or something?" he asked, throwing Zell off.

"What?" Zell asked, his brow bunching in a fierce glower. "Just what the hell are you implying?"

"Nothing. Just curious as to why you're ready to crucify Cassi even though there's evidence to the contrary that leads straight to Vissher."

"That's a load of horseshit and I'm your superior so watch your mouth."

"I'd like to have Olivia Nolan's body exhumed and tested for arsenic poison."

"Why?"

"Because information I gathered in Virginia Beach supports the theory that Vissher isn't who he says he is. I have information stating that Vissher was actually married before to another wealthy woman under a different name. Funny thing is, she died under suspicious circumstances."

Zell looked perplexed with Thomas's information and Thomas sensed a crack so he pushed. "Listen, we've got a guy who seems adept at smoke and mirrors and you know the best way to take the heat off of yourself is to put it someplace else. I think Cassi got too close to the truth and that's why he trumped up these charges. He paid those women to make a false statement and now one is dead. The other one is alive only because we discovered the contaminated food before she ate it."

Zell took a long moment before responding. Then he said, "Get a court order and exhume the body but keep it quiet. The last thing I need is Lionel Visssher in my office making waves over this until I have more to go on. In the meantime, your friend can stay here."

That wouldn't work. Knowing Cassi she'd find a way to skip town and then the trouble would start all over. "Release her to me," he suggested.

Zell scowled. "Have you lost your mind? No."

"Look, you and I know that we don't have much to hold her on, given the new evidence, but if you release her into my custody I will make sure she stays in town."

Zell considered this, then barked, "Fine. But she's wearing an ankle bracelet. You may be soft on the woman but I don't trust that she's not a criminal herself."

"A thief is not a murderer," he said to Zell. "You have my word that I will bring her back if the evidence doesn't support my theory."

"You willing to stake your credentials on this woman?" he asked.

Thomas didn't hesitate. "Yes."

He believed her. In his heart, he knew Cassi was innocent.

He just hoped to God he wasn't putting his trust where it didn't belong. There was a whisper of a voice telling him to be careful but he was way past able to give it heed.

He wondered if his father had had a similar voice going off in his head right before he lost his mind and killed his family.

Thomas shuddered and shoved it all away.

He had other things to worry about at the moment.

CASSI PACED THE TIGHT quarters of the holding cell, about ready to jump out of her skin. She'd known coming here was a bad idea, right up there with skydiving without a parachute or buying seafood from the trunk of someone's car.

She'd believed him and the asshole had served her up like a noonday meal to his superior. She was hot—so angry that she was fairly certain she could melt metal with her eyes—but there was more than anger simmering under the surface. She felt betrayed. And that was infinitely worse.

Tears pricked her eyes and she dashed them away, angry at their appearance. She felt weak and pathetic and needy. Three things she despised.

The door opened and she stopped abruptly to stare at Tommy as he entered. She glared. "What do you want?"

"C'mon," he said, gesturing. "We're getting out of here."

His statement threw her. "What do you mean? They're just letting me go?"

"More or less," he said, but he was holding something in his hands.

"What's that?"

"A new accessory," he quipped, but she didn't find it funny, especially when she realized what it was. She wasn't amused at all. He exhaled loudly and she was incensed that he had the gall to be annoyed. "Listen, work with me here. I had to make a deal. In order to let you out on your own recognizance, you have to wear a GPS bracelet. It's not a big deal."

She eyed him coldly. "Then you wear it."

"I'm not the one in trouble."

She glared and looked away but after stewing for a minute she lifted her pant leg and thrust her foot at him. "Fine. But don't think for a second that I'm happy about this," she warned him, looking away as he clicked the latch in place, securing the bracelet and officially putting her on the FBI's radar. "Great. Now the U.S. government can find me no matter where I go, whether it's to the grocery store or to the toilet."

"Having tracked you for the past two months I'd say that's a blessing. Especially around bathrooms," he teased, but she wasn't ready to forgive him. He sighed and gestured. "Let's get out of here. You're in my custody until further notice."

"What else is new?" she retorted, sending him a dark look. "And if you think I'm sleeping handcuffed to you again you're crazy."

He gave her a sideways glance that heated her blood in spite of how pissed she was, and he warned in a low tone that sent goose bumps across her skin, "If I put you in handcuffs again...you won't be sleeping."

She gasped and stalked past him. "Keep dreaming, Tommy boy," she growled. "Keep dreaming!"

MAYBE HIS RELIEF WAS premature but he was just glad to have Cassi out of that cell and back with him. He knew their problems weren't over but given how dangerous Lionel Vissher seemed and the fact that no one but them seemed to realize this made him edgy. Call him a Neanderthal but he preferred to keep Cassi close for her own protection. Of course, he had to laugh at that sentiment because Cassi was plenty able to take care of herself. But it was the way he felt and he wasn't inclined to spend too much time analyzing it.

"Where are we going?" she asked, as they pulled out of the Bureau parking lot. Her arms were crossed over her chest and every now and again she glanced down at the bracelet in disgust. His chances of a pleasant evening were dwindling so he figured he'd take her to the one place she was sure to behave herself.

"First, my apartment here in Pittsburgh, then Mama Jo's. It's only about two hours from here."

She turned to stare at him, then she stammered an emphatic, *"No."*

"Why not? You used to love Mama Jo and I know the feeling was mutual. Besides if she finds out that you were in town and didn't stop in…she'll turn me inside out."

"I don't want to see her," Cassi said, but there was fear in her voice that he didn't understand. "Take me to a hotel."

"What's going on?" he asked.

She refused to answer. Her mouth pinched and she appeared mutinously silent.

He pulled over to the shoulder, startling her, and demanded to know what was wrong. When he received nothing, he was perplexed. "What did Mama Jo do to upset you like this? She thought the world of you."

"I know that," she said.

"So?"

She whirled to face him, tears sparkling in her eyes. "So I don't want to see her disappointment. Don't you think I deal with enough of that on my own just by looking in the mirror? I can't deal with Mama Jo's disappointment, too. I know you probably told her about the last time we saw each other. I said some bad things and some of it was insulting to Mama Jo and I hate that of myself. I just don't know if I can handle seeing her right now."

Thomas was floored by her admission. He recalled that night. She'd been partying pretty hard. She'd called him to come and get her from a party. She'd been strung out on cocaine and whatever else had been floating around the place. But when he'd gotten there she'd changed her mind and didn't want to leave.

He'd been pissed. Not only at her actions, begging him to come out there at 3:00 a.m., but her actions up to that point, too. She'd been sliding further and further from the person he knew into this drugged-out socialite mess who drank too much, partied too hard and refused to take responsibility for anything. Her so-called friends were no different, which was why he refused to have anything to do with them. He'd yelled at her and tried to drag her into the car. She'd refused. And in her mental state she'd said a few harsh things about his childhood and his foster mother.

Looking across at her, seeing her obvious shame, he realized he'd forgiven her a long time ago. He knew that hadn't been her saying those things. But he could see that she was a long way away from forgiving herself. He also knew that until she faced her shame and dealt with it, it would never go away. The best way to do that was with tough love. "Well, then, this is a perfect opportunity to get it off your chest," he said, ignoring her outraged groan. "You have to deal with it sooner or later. Sooner, in my experience, is better than later. Besides, I already called and let her know that after I picked up a few things we'd be on our way."

"You're a sonofabitch, Thomas Bristol," she shouted. "You can't force someone to deal with their issues just because it fits within your time schedule. You're a stubborn mule of a man, you know that? Hardheaded, too," she spat.

"As hardheaded as the woman beside me." He

laughed when she turned away from him. Hopefully, Mama Jo had hot corn bread waiting. Cassi had always been a fan of Mama's cooking.

CHAPTER FOURTEEN

THE TWO-STORY APARTMENT complex was everything Cassi imagined Tommy would look for in a place he used to simply shower and sleep.

It was nice without being fussy, gated to keep out the riffraff and perfectly utilitarian.

"Decent place," she noted, her gaze bouncing over the manicured lawns that in spite of the winter were still green and lush. Perhaps they were fake, she mused.

"Thanks." He pulled into a parking spot and exited to open her door.

He led her to the second floor of the unit closest to them and unlocked the door. The air smelled like musty apartment, as if no one had lived there in months. It was bare, with little on the walls, and lacking in personality. She wrinkled her nose. "Your decorating style stinks," she announced.

Caught off guard, he closed the door behind them and locked it, probably from habit. "What do you mean?" he asked.

She gestured to the room. "This. It's so boring.

Where's the pizzazz? The signature style that says, 'This is my space. Love it or leave it'?"

"This is rich coming from the woman whose decorating style from what I could see in New York was abject squalor."

"Hey, that wasn't my style. That was just what was available in my price range. What's your excuse?"

"I don't care that much about that stuff. It's just a place to—"

"Sleep and eat?" she supplied for him, and he nodded.

"Exactly. And since I've been trailing you for the past two months, I haven't had much reason to hang out here. Besides, some weekends I drive to Bridgeport to spend time with Mama Jo so she's not all alone."

His concern for Mama Jo warmed her heart but she didn't let it show. She simply tucked it away in a private place where all the rest of her true feelings for Tommy resided.

He gestured toward the bedroom. "I'll be right back. I just need some fresh clothes and then we'll be on our way."

"Take your time," she muttered, not the least bit ready to face Mama Jo. Heavens, she'd almost do anything to avoid that homecoming. She was ashamed of her past behavior, and Mama Jo was the only one who could make her feel the burn of it.

She wandered to the kitchen and opened the fridge. Empty except for a few beers. Talk about a bachelor pad. She opened his cabinets and peered inside. A whole lot of boxed macaroni and cheese met her eye. He'd always loved the stuff, though Mama Jo swore it would probably cause a brain lesion or something equally horrible with all the preservatives. Cassi had been surprised Mama Jo even let it into her house when they were kids. She was of the homemade persuasion when it came to cooking. In fact, the foundation of what Cassi knew how to make came from Mama Jo's kitchen. "I'm gonna tell on you," she chortled to herself about the macaroni and cheese. Maybe she could deflect the attention from her to Tommy.

Meandering from the kitchen she moved down the short hallway and peered into the guest bedroom, which he'd turned into a small workout center. That explained the chiseled abs she found most delightful and distracting.

She took a left and entered his bedroom. Goose pimples rioted along her forearms as she found him standing there stripped and changing into a fresh set of clothes.

"I know a way to spice up this room," she noted casually, trailing her fingers over his neatly made bed.

He grabbed a shirt from his drawer and looked

away to find a pair of socks. "I can only imagine..." But as he turned to face her, his jaw went slack as she'd completely divested herself of her clothing and was standing there nude.

"What are you doing?" he asked, his gaze feasting on her every curve. "We don't have time..."

Her mouth lifted in a playful smile. "Darling, have you never heard of the quickie? I'm sure we have plenty of time."

A feral grin split his face. "Hell, yeah," he growled, dropping his shirt so it landed in a heap on the floor as he tackled her on the bed. She squealed in delight, her fingers dancing along his waistband, eager to pull him from his jeans. He cupped her breasts and buried his face against the soft flesh, pressing fevered kisses to the sensitive skin. "You're a bad influence on me, I think," he murmured right before sucking a tight, budded nipple into his hot mouth.

"I know," she admitted, not the least bit sorry. "But as bad influences go...I'm pretty good, wouldn't you say?"

He answered with his mouth...everywhere.

Cassi sank into the bed and lost herself in the feel of being totally possessed by a man who was obsessed with her pleasure first and wondered if it were possible to keep him in her bed, perpetually sidetracked for the rest of their lives. Her sigh turned into a moan as he put her legs over his shoulders and plunged so deep she nearly saw stars. He rode her hard, drawing out an orgasm so intense she lost her breath, and she was sure her heart stopped.

"Tommy," she said, when she could finally speak, wrapping her arms around him as tightly as she could, reveling in the feel of their hearts beating frantically together.

"Yeah, babe," he managed to say as he rested his sweat-dampened forehead against hers.

"Let me know when you're ready for round two."

He looked up to gauge if she were serious and when she grinned up at him, he rolled until she was on top, her mound resting slickly atop his already-thickening shaft, his grin matching hers. "I'm ready when you are, sweetheart."

And Cassi reveled in the fun of the sequel of a not-so-quick quickie and the art of avoiding emotional quicksand.

If it were possible, Cassi would've sunk into the upholstery of the car and disappeared before they arrived at Mama Jo's, but as they pulled up to the house, the white clapboard siding gleaming in the dim moonlight, Cassi knew she had nowhere to run. She'd have to face the diminutive woman and deal with whatever fallout there may be.

Tommy gave her a reassuring grin as he said,

"Don't worry, she doesn't bite. But she may lecture you a bit." At Cassi's look of distress, he laughed. "I can't believe this. You look ready to throw up. It's not going to be that bad. She'll mostly be happy to see you. I promise."

Cassi swallowed. Maybe he was right. Mama Jo had always had a big heart. She'd have to to become a foster parent and then willingly adopt three of the boys with the worst personal histories. Just from their backgrounds alone, the boys screamed "head cases" but she'd handled each one with a grace and skill that defied logic. In truth, Cassi had always secretly been in awe of the small black woman.

Tommy walked up the stairs and she trailed behind him. He knocked once and then walked in like he owned the place because this was his childhood sanctuary and Mama Jo didn't stand on ceremony.

The minute she stepped over the threshold and the familiar smells of the old farmhouse assailed her nostrils, the memories popped up sharp and vibrant. She could close her eyes and see herself sitting over by the black potbellied stove where Mama Jo would have a kettle chirping to keep moisture in the air and coffee percolating at all hours because you never knew when guests might arrive. Mama Jo had Southern hospitality ingrained in her bones. She believed in two things with the fervor of a devout Christian. One, always offer a guest coffee or sweet tea; and two, a home-cooked meal would solve most problems.

She was the black version of Paula Dean, and Cassi had always secretly wished that she'd been born in a house like Mama Jo's instead of her own. What Mama Jo didn't have in material items she made up for with love and plenty of good food.

And right now, Cassi was terrified of how Mama's opinion of her may have been damaged from her actions so long ago.

"We're here," Tommy hollered, his voice ringing through the house.

"Come on in and close the door behind you so we don't catch our death from a draft," a voice said, floating in from the kitchen area.

Tommy did as instructed and they headed toward the back of the house. The scuffed and worn floorboards groaned under their weight, making it impossible to sneak up on anyone in this house, and they entered the kitchen.

Myriad savory smells filled the warm room, and there was Mama Jo, stirring a pot of something and gesturing at Tommy to come and kiss her cheek, which he hastened to do. Then she turned to Cassi and she gave her a good long look over the top of her glasses. Cassi felt stripped to the bone with that sharp gaze. The woman could probably work for the government in interrogation. She hadn't said a word yet but Cassi had the overwhelming need to confess every little dirty secret she held to her breast.

But then Mama Jo returned to her pot and without commenting on anything from the past, said to Cassi, "Well, now, don't just stand there, missy. You know where the plates are. Do you remember how to set a proper table?"

She blinked and then stammered, shooting an unsure glance at Tommy, "Yes, ma'am, I do."

Mama Jo nodded approvingly. "Well, then what you waitin' for, honey? We can't eat this dinner in our laps now can we? Grab the soup bowls, too." Then she turned to Tommy. "Make yourself useful and go get the sweet tea from the outside refrigerator, son."

Tommy winked at Cassi and went to do as requested, leaving the two women alone. Going from memory, Cassi went to the cabinet and grabbed the plates and flatware. Aside from the sound of whatever was bubbling in the pot and simmering on the stove, there was nothing but silence. Cassi kept waiting for Mama Jo to say something, but she didn't. She kept whatever she was thinking to herself and it was driving Cassi crazy. Frankly, she'd rather the woman berate her up one side and down the other for being such a screwup than suffer the silence.

"You look good, Mama Jo," Cassi offered tentatively, placing the bowls on the table.

"Mmm-hmm," was all she said to that. "Brown isn't your color, child. Hand me that bowl, please. I can't quite reach it." Cassi reached the bowl on the top shelf and handed it to Mama Jo. "Seems you've been up to all sorts of mischief, I hear."

Her cheeks burned and she glanced around for Tommy. Where the hell did he go for that sweet tea? The neighboring county? "Uh, well, a little. I'm trying to make things right, though."

Mama Jo nodded and ladled the thick stew into the bowl and handed it to Cassi to put on the table. Then she pulled fresh biscuits from the oven and put them in a red gingham bread basket. She handed the basket to Cassi just as Tommy returned carrying the pitcher of sweet tea. "Ah, there we go. Nothing fancy tonight, just good old-fashioned stuff that'll stick to your ribs for a time. Come on, now, take a seat and let's catch up."

A wide smile wreathed the older woman's face and a pang of wistful longing followed. When Mama Jo took someone into her heart she didn't let them go easily. Her love was fierce and generous but Cassi felt she'd forfeited that privilege the day she said those awful things. Tears pricked her eyes and Mama Jo, sharp as ever, caught the glitter before she could wipe it away.

"Have a biscuit, Cassi honey," she instructed, passing the biscuit basket. "There's nothing that's so bad that can't be fixed with fresh butter melting on a hot biscuit." She took a biscuit herself and tore it apart to slather it with butter. A bite later, after she'd slowly chewed and enjoyed a very perfect biscuit, she said, "Now, tell me about this trouble you're in."

TOMMY SAT AND FILLED HIS belly while Cassi reluctantly brought Mama Jo up to speed on her current situation.

Cassi finished by jerking up her pant leg and showing the anklet. "And now I have to wear this stupid thing like a damn dog or something. It's humiliating."

"It's temporary and you should be grateful that you're not sitting in the holding cell," Tommy reminded her but Cassi was having none of it.

Her fire returning, she said, "Yeah, well if I hadn't let you talk me into turning myself in I'd be anklet-free with my dignity intact."

"Your dignity is just fine," Tommy grumbled, a little annoyed that she wasn't even the slightest bit willing to see how he'd put himself on the line to secure her freedom.

Mama Jo's eyes danced as she listened to the two of them spar and for a second it felt like old times. Cassi had often showed up at Mama Jo's when they were kids. Cassi had loved the simple home with its well-trodden floors that spoke of countless little feet that had echoed through the single-story farmhouse. This was a house filled with so much love the porch bowed in certain spots. Once Mama Jo had adopted "her boys" she'd resigned her spot in the social services roster saying she had her hands full with him, Christian and Owen. In spite of being a privileged princess who was accustomed to maids and a nanny, Cassi had fit right in with the eclectic group.

"How are your brothers doing?" Cassi asked, breaking into his thoughts and changing the subject. "I thought about stopping in to see Christian while I was in New York but I hadn't quite figured out how to do that without tipping you or any other law enforcement who might've been looking for me."

"He's doing good. Making money hand over fist in that fancy Manhattan bar." He looked to Mama Jo. "He told me to tell you that he loves and misses you. No one makes bread pudding like you. Not even in any of those rich restaurants, he said."

Mama Jo warmed under the praise but her mouth pursed. "That boy…such a sweet talker. Next time you talk to him you tell him a phone call wouldn't break the bank now and then." She sighed. "I wish he'd come home once in a while. I know he's doing good but I worry about him around all those city girls. He's got a soft heart you know," she said, and Thomas rolled his eyes.

"You've always babied him," he said, but there was no true rivalry there. Christian was a year younger than both him and Owen but the kid had probably seen more of the gritty side of life than either of them had before he hit the tender age of five. "He's fine," he assured her.

"And what about Owen?" Cassi asked.

"Stressed. He's dealing with some kind of environmental group that's out to shut down his logging operation. It's driving him nuts. But you know Owen…he'll come through. He's as stubborn and hardheaded as someone else I know."

Cassi gave him a look that said "Ha, ha" and got up to help Mama Jo clear the table.

"I'll never understand why he had to go so far away," Mama Jo said, shaking her head. "They have trees right here in West Virginia. No need to run off to the wilds of California."

Cassi laughed softly. "Owen hates to shovel snow. He probably figured he'd never have to shovel snow again if he moved away from the East Coast."

They all chuckled at that and Thomas felt the tension flow from his body. The events from the past few days faded and he could almost forget that there was a mess still waiting for them.

Almost.

Mama Jo served up some cobbler she made from

peaches she'd frozen earlier in the summer and then they moved to the living room.

"Cassi, where are you staying, honey?" Mama Jo asked.

Cassi's gaze darted to him and he interjected, "With me. She's in my custody."

Mama Jo's mouth turned down in a frown. "That's not proper. She's not your wife. Not yet anyway," she added, and Thomas nearly jumped at her assumption. He started to say something to the contrary but she shushed him and patted Cassi's hand. "You can stay here in Tommy's old bedroom. Besides, I could use the company now that my boys are all grown-up and have forgotten where home is."

Cassi smiled and shot him a triumphant look before saying, "I'd love to stay here with you, Mama Jo. Thank you for offering."

But there was no way he was letting Cassi out of his sight. He didn't trust her not to sneak out in the middle of the night, which would not only make major problems for him on the job front but it would crack Mama Jo's heart, and that's one thing he couldn't abide.

"Sorry, Mama, that's generous but I can't let her do that. She's with me or she has to go back to the holding cell."

Mama Jo gave him a quizzical look. "Boy, this is Cassi we're talking about. She isn't no criminal and you know that. Stop treating her like one. It's bad enough she's got that fool anklet on. She doesn't need you acting like her warden."

Laughter danced in Cassi's eyes and if he hadn't felt like he'd been reduced to a teenager by Mama Jo's scolding tone he might've chuckled at her defense of "poor Cassi."

"Mama, it's not that simple. She's in my custody. My job is on the line and I can't take the risk that she'll bail in the middle of the night."

At that, the mirth faded from Cassi's eyes and she looked away, plainly hurt by his admission that she was basically untrustworthy. A flash of guilt made him defensive. What did she expect? There were major issues they had to deal with and while she may be innocent of some things, she was certainly guilty of others. But he could tell by the compression of Mama Jo's lips that she was displeased with his statement. He shifted under that disapproving stare but before he could try to explain, Cassi rose and excused herself to the bathroom. He rose automatically and Cassi stopped him with a cutting stare. "I know the way and if I recall, the bathroom window is too small for me to fit through," she snapped, and then left him feeling like an ass.

He fell into his chair with a heavy sigh. "Why am I the bad guy here?" he muttered to no one in particular. Then he turned to Mama Jo. "She escaped through a bathroom window the first time I tried to capture her. So it's not far-fetched…" he started mulishly, but Mama Jo just shook her head, disappointment in her eyes.

"You've loved that woman all your life," she stated. "And the way you're treating her is beneath you."

"I'm not the one who broke the law," he stated, matter-of-fact.

She nodded. "Yes, she admits to making some mistakes but I'd like to know how well you'd handle having your life tipped upside down without a soul to care if you lived or died."

He met Mama's gaze. "I have. Remember?"

She disagreed. "No. You had me. Cassi was kicked out of the nest without so much as a penny to her name by a man who she believes killed her mother. And the one person she should've been able to turn to has treated her like a criminal. Shame on you, Thomas. I thought I raised you better than that."

"Mama—"

"Don't *Mama* me. I know what's going on here and it doesn't take a genius to see it. You're punishing her for something that happened long ago when you were both too young to know what matters in life."

"That's not true," he protested but there was

something in the back of his mind that contradicted his words and he was afraid to look at it too closely for fear that it might be real. "She turned into a different person. You don't know who she is now."

Mama Jo disagreed. "No, Thomas. I don't know who *you* are right now."

"What was I supposed to do?" he demanded, his tone raising a faint eyebrow in the face he'd come to associate with love and acceptance. The fact that he was getting a verbal ass-whoopin' at his age was rubbing him wrong. Even if he deserved it. "Wasn't it better that it was me? I could've handed the case off to someone else and right now she'd be facing charges for crimes she didn't commit. But I didn't walk away like I should've."

"I'm not going to argue with you," she stated, withdrawing and tucking a warm wool lap blanket around her birdlike legs. "If you believe you treated her with the kindness deserved of your friendship, I have nothing more to say about it. But I will add this…you're not dragging her from here to creation like some kind of rag doll. You can take the couch and she'll sleep in your room. And that's all I'm going to say about it."

Thomas bit back a few swear words. There was no arguing with her when she dug her heels in like this. And while he appreciated that she was doing what she thought was right for Cassi…the selfish part of him was angry that Mama Jo had taken her side.

And there was the other part of him—an unmentionable part—that was more than disappointed that he'd be taking the couch, far away from the perfect fit of Cassi's body against his. Although, as mad as Cassi was at him, he suspected the only touch he'd get from her at this point would inflict sharp pain on his groin.

"Fine," he ground out. "But if she sneaks out in the middle of the night, don't say I didn't warn you."

"Don't be such a bear," she chastised him, adding as another thought came to her. "Oh, goodness, I nearly forgot—that Lionel Vissher character came to visit, looking for Cassi a few weeks ago. I didn't trust him. He seemed like a snake oil salesman to me."

"What did he say?"

"Not much. Tried to say he was worried about her and that he wondered if I'd had any contact with her. Of course, I hadn't but even if I had I wouldn't have told him. Like I said, there was something about the man I just didn't like."

Thomas grinned in spite of his earlier irritation at Mama's defense of Cassi. "Did you shoo him off the porch with your broom?" he teased.

She frowned. "No, but I wanted to. Anyway, is

there any reason he'd be looking for her all of a sudden?"

Thomas's smile faded. "Yeah. He probably wants to make sure she stops asking questions that he doesn't want answered."

"Because Cassi believes he killed her mother," Mama Jo surmised, and he nodded. Her mouth tightened with resolve. "I knew that man was up to no good."

"Whoa, Mama, we don't know that for sure... Cassi has some compelling circumstantial evidence but nothing concrete. And don't forget, Cassi isn't exactly the best at telling the truth these days. We can't simply take her word for it."

Mama Jo pinned him with a short stare. "*You* can't take her word. I believe her just fine. If she says that man is bad, I believe her. You ought to try it yourself. It might clear up a whole lot of that garbage you've got clogging up your brain."

He wanted to groan but he wouldn't be so disrespectful. Besides, once Mama got something into her head it would take dynamite to dislodge it. "All right, Mama. You've made your point."

And damn if he didn't feel that point digging into his side, making it impossible to ignore.

CHAPTER FIFTEEN

CASSI HAD OVERHEARD BITS of the conversation between Mama Jo and Tommy while she was in the bathroom. The sharp whack of the front door shutting behind Tommy made Cassi bite her lip and sigh heavily. He was pissed and probably a little embarrassed. Served him right, she thought, but the righteousness faded as she recalled she'd brought this turmoil to his life. She knew how close Tommy and Mama Jo were. She didn't like to think that she was at the center of their disagreement. "I'm sorry, Tommy," she murmured. But it was too late. They were both knee-deep in whatever was going to happen.

She returned to the living room and before she could say anything, Mama Jo gestured toward the door. "He's probably sulking on the porch. Why don't you go and see if he's willing to calm down and start acting like a grown-up."

"Don't be too hard on him, Mama Jo," Cassi said. "He didn't ask for this mess. He's just trying to do what's best."

"Best for who?" Mama Jo queried, eyeing her intently. "Certainly not what's best for himself and not what's best for you. So I ask again…"

Cassi stopped her. "I'll go talk to him. He's a good man, Mama Jo. You did right by him."

Mama Jo's weathered face softened in a warm smile. "Yes, I did," she agreed with pride in her voice. "All my boys turned out all right. Now go and get him before he catches pneumonia."

Cassi grabbed her coat and headed outside. Her breath plumed in the frosty night air and she shivered as she slid on her coat. She spotted Tommy sitting on the porch swing, staring at the cracked pine boards on the floor in the dim glow of the lamplight. The swing creaked as she took a seat beside him and gazed up at the stars. Neither spoke and the silence sat between them, filled with the weight of everything they ought to say to one another.

Finally, Tommy said, "Mama Jo's right." Cassi held her breath, wondering which part he was referring to. He looked up and met her questioning gaze. "I've loved you my entire life."

His blunt admission sucked the air from her lungs. Somehow, she'd known that, even though they'd never said the words. He'd never been the kind of man who spouted off pretty things or gave in to overt displays of affection. He'd been her solid friend—her best friend—always willing to stand in the background so she could have the spotlight. But then she'd ruined everything and his absence had left her feeling adrift.

He'd been her anchor.

"I wish I'd been smart enough to love you the way you loved me," she said, imagining how her life would've been different. "But I wasn't and I made big mistakes, Tommy. I know there's a part of you that's angry with me for changing into someone you don't like. But I can't change what I did. Only what I will do in the future."

"How do I know you're not going to split the minute things get hot?" he asked.

She drew a deep breath. How to answer that? She didn't know herself. "I don't know," she answered truthfully. "But all I can tell you is that if I have to put my trust in someone, you're it. I won't lie. I'm scared. And there's still a chance this could all blow up in our faces. What then? I don't know. I guess we'll find out, right?"

He nodded but his face held a faint grimace as if he were struggling. "I hate this," he admitted, meeting her gaze. "I've never been so conflicted before. You bring chaos and I don't know if I like it."

She should appreciate his honesty but it hurt. Was he saying that he didn't know if he wanted her around once everything was settled? She blinked back an unexpected wash of tears. Ouch. "You have to do what's right for you," was all she could say—all she could trust herself to say.

He grunted a response. "Yeah."

She turned to him. "But for what it's worth…I am glad it was you. Even if I've done a terrible job of showing it."

They held each other's stare for several seconds before they leaned in and pressed their cold lips together for a tender, featherlight kiss that was as tentative yet heartfelt as anything she could've conveyed with her words.

She just hoped he heard what she was saying.

THOMAS FOLLOWED CASSI into the house. Mama Jo had retired but she'd left him a pile of blankets for the couch. He sighed and Cassi smiled, reading his thoughts as easily as if they were scrolling across his forehead. "Someone has to make sure I remain a lady," she teased before disappearing into the bedroom with a kiss blown his way.

Thomas rolled out the blankets and made his bed. He knew it would be a long time before sleep found him, which was a damn shame because that meant he'd spend that time thinking and he really wasn't in the mood to think.

He replayed the conversations with Mama Jo and Cassi in his head and realized something he hadn't before this moment. He'd always thought he was pretty well-adjusted in spite of his past. He left the night terrors behind when he turned thirteen; he stopped waking up with tears on his pillow at fourteen. He rediscovered laughter and happiness with his new family.

But there were things he still couldn't do.

He couldn't look at pictures of his parents or his little brother, TJ.

He couldn't help the tic that twitched in his eye when he dealt with men who beat women.

And he couldn't fathom the idea of marrying anyone without breaking out in a sweat.

So maybe he wasn't as well-adjusted as he thought.

Thomas rolled to his back and stared at the ceiling.

Quiet times like this he could still hear the gunshots ringing in his ears.

He could hear his father's drunken rage, and seconds before the final shot, his anguish.

He could remember the bruises on his mother before that night. Something always managed to set his dad off and his mom would pay the price. But she'd tried to make it work. She'd tell Thomas, "Marriage isn't easy and I'm no quitter," even when she was holding a bag of frozen peas to her eye or busted lip, whatever was battered and bruised that day.

And then there was *that* night.

Thomas squeezed his eyes shut and pushed the memory away but tonight it wouldn't budge.

His mother's screams echoed off the kitchen walls while Thomas and TJ huddled in their beds, flinching at every crash and bang, and the shattering of glass.

Why hadn't she run? Why hadn't she told the cops about the abuse? So many questions he'd never get to ask because that night was the night Becky Bristol was taken out of the game.

Along with eight-year-old TJ.

Thomas would've joined his family if it hadn't been for the fact that he'd run from his bedroom to call 911 and then hid under his parents' bed when his father had busted into the bedroom. TJ had begged him not to leave. He could still hear his voice, pleading. And then the cries, "Daddy, please…"

Two shots later, Thomas was an orphan.

His heartrate accelerated and sweat popped along his hairline. He was not his father. He would never do such horrible things. *Never.* But who really knows what they're capable of until they're pushed to the edge of reason? Surely his father hadn't woken up that morning and said, "I'm going to go on a bender and then come home and kill my family in a drunken rage over some imagined fault."

No, he was fairly certain his father had not said that. Or thought it.

But did it matter? He did it. And Thomas was all that was left of the Bristol family who once lived in a modest home on Olive Street where the neighbors were friendly and the paperboy never threw your paper into the hedges but nice and even, right where it belonged.

Okay, maybe it hadn't been that perfect but in the mind of a twelve-year-old boy...it'd been home.

For a brief horrifying second, he could almost understand his father's insanity. But then Cassi had hit the nail on the head. Love wasn't cruel or possessive. And his father had been both at his worst.

He let out a pent-up breath and was startled to realize his fists had been clenched. He shook them loose and took a few deep breaths to clear his head.

He was not his father.

He was not his father.

He was not his father.

Maybe if he said it enough times he'd lose the fear that shadowed him, unwelcome and sinister, lurking and waiting to jump out at him when he least expected it.

Maybe.

Too bad *maybe* wasn't good enough.

CASSI AWOKE FROM THE MOST delicious dream, curled in a cocoon of warmth under the handmade quilt covering her. She stretched and yawned, a sleepy smile forming without thought.

"That's something I could get used to seeing every day."

Tommy's voice snapped her to awareness and she rose up on her elbows to find Tommy watching her with a soft yet hungry expression. Her toes curled under the blankets and she was hit by a wave of desire that was all the more potent for her inability to do anything about it. She burrowed into the blankets and told him, "Come back with coffee or tea or something reasonably caffeinated and we'll talk. Until then…hit the road."

He chuckled and she grinned from the safety of her blanket fortress. As mornings went, today wasn't starting off half-bad.

AFTER A HEARTY BREAKFAST that was sure to put a few pounds on her backside—which was precisely the point, as Mama Jo had stated quite emphatically when she'd seen how thin Cassie had become—they returned to the Bureau at the request of Director Zell.

That guy made Cassi nervous. And she wasn't sure it was entirely because he'd been ready and willing to throw her in a cell and lose the key.

He looked perplexed and more than a little bothered when they entered his office.

"So, it seems you might be on to something," Zell admitted, looking about as happy as someone who'd just been given acupuncture with a nail gun. "Forensics turned up arsenic in the food sample you collected at the home of that Jones woman. We managed to turn up a private investigator who made the contact with the two women. He said he was paid in cash to talk these women into making the false statements. He also said he never met the guy who paid him. The money was left in an airport locker for him to pick up."

"Smart," Thomas said with a frown. "So now what?"

Zell sighed heavily and pinched his nose with two stubbed fingers. "We've got a court order to exhume Ms. Olivia Nolan. The crews are probably already at the cemetery. We also have enough now for a search warrant for Vissher's property but given how long ago these deaths occurred, I'm not holding out much hope of finding anything of use."

"You never know. Sometimes people get arrogant," Thomas said, sending a quick look Cassi's way. He felt rather than saw her involuntary shake over her mother's exhumation. It was what she'd wanted, but being faced with the reality that her mother was being ripped from her final resting place was more than a little upsetting. But when he glanced at her, she was dry-eyed and focused. "When will you know anything?" she asked.

Zell didn't look compelled to answer her but he did. "I've put a rush on this case...we should have the forensics in about a week."

"That long?" she asked, plainly disappointed, but she nodded. "Okay. Are you going to bring Lionel in for questioning?"

Zell shook his head. "Not yet. Not until we have some solid evidence. All we have right now is circumstantial. Just stay put and you'll hear soon enough what's happening." He looked to Thomas. "I assume you can handle keeping her out of trouble until then?"

"I'm not an errant child, Mr. Zell," Cassi said, stiffening, and Thomas didn't blame her. "But I might caution you about Lionel Vissher. It's likely he's already getting ready to skip town if he knows about the exhumation. If I were you I'd put a man on him for the time being."

"He's not going anywhere," Zell grumbled, looking away.

"How do you know?" Cassi challenged, frustration lacing her voice. "He's a slippery bastard and you don't know how easily he can disappear, especially with plenty of resources."

"Thank you for your advice, Ms. Nolan. I have no doubt you're an expert on how a person can disappear, but suffice it to say we know what we're doing."

Cassi shot Thomas a look filled with annoyance and muttered something about a "pigheaded suit with a gun" and stalked from the room.

"She's right. If Lionel splits, it'll be hard to find him. We already know from Cassi that he'd been stockpiling money when Olivia was alive. For all we know he's got enough to disappear and live quite comfortably for years."

"You just worry about keeping the flight risk grounded and I'll take care of the rest," Zell said, dismissing him.

"What aren't you telling me?" Thomas asked quietly. It wasn't like Zell to act like this and it was setting off all sorts of alarms and whistles.

Zell glowered at him. "Since when is it okay for you to question me? I'm your superior. I think you'd better reevaluate your tone and attitude, Agent Bristol. Now, get the hell out of here and back to work. You want to put this guy away so badly, go find me some real evidence and not something that starts with 'I have a feeling…' because we sure as hell can't convict someone with a *feeling*."

Thomas bit back a hot retort and nodded stiffly. "You can find me on my cell," he said, and Zell waved him out of the office.

Zell had never been accused of being a people

person but he was sure working overtime on that Grouchiest Boss Alive award.

He rejoined Cassi in the hall. "So, what's his problem? Is it me or is he just an asshole on most days?" she asked.

"I don't know. I was just wondering that myself," he answered, but didn't want to dwell on the subject when they had plenty more to worry about than Zell's bad attitude. "Listen, are you okay about the exhumation? I know it can't be easy for you."

She rubbed her palms on her arms and shrugged but he saw the hurt in her eyes. She caught his knowing stare and offered a short, unsure laugh even as she wiped a tear away from the corner of her eye. "I don't know. I thought I'd be fine with it. I mean, I know that's not her in that box. Her spirit is long gone but I hate the idea of pulling her body out of the ground."

"That's understandable. Don't worry, it'll be done with the utmost care and consideration. I'll make sure of it."

She smiled her gratitude and he so wanted to wrap her in his arms and protect her from the world, but that wasn't a good idea standing here in the Bureau lobby with so many eyes on them. He exhaled softly and gestured to the front doors. "Let's get out of here and take a drive around the old haunts."

"Really?" she asked. "It's not exactly good driving weather out there."

He glanced in the direction of the ominous, dark clouds threatening a deluge of rain later and he shrugged. "What's a little rain? C'mon, this place is depressing enough as it is. No need to hang out any longer than we need to, right?"

She peered at him and when she saw that he was serious, her face broke into a smile as she agreed with a nod. "Right. Last I checked I don't melt," she said.

He winked. "Good to know."

CHAPTER SIXTEEN

CASSI WASN'T SURE WHAT Tommy was up to, but she suspected he was just trying to keep her mind occupied on anything other than the fact that a crew was ripping into the earth where her mother was laid to rest, with the intent of taking a few DNA samples from her corpse. He seemed to know that she'd never truly dealt with her grief over losing her mom and he was trying to be there for her. It was hard not to fall a little bit harder for him at that moment even if she knew it was ill-advised. Theirs was not bound to be a happy ending. She tried to remember that but it was tough when he was acting like the man he'd always been—caring, supportive and solid.

They drove past Winston High and parked across the street. School was in session so only a few students were walking the grounds. Other than a few superficial changes in the landscaping, the school looked as it had when they were students.

"Wow. Talk about a time warp," she remarked wistfully, catching his light chuckle. "It's easy to remember what it was like being a student there when everything looks the same."

"Remember that time when Cindy Hawthorne had set her sights on you for the winter formal?" Cassi asked, grinning at the memory of Thomas trying to avoid her in the halls just so he didn't have to hurt her feelings by turning her down. "Oh, man, she had it for you bad. But then, so did most of the girls in our graduating class."

"You're exaggerating," he said, but his cheeks flared an adorable shade of pink. Tommy had never been comfortable being the object of so much attention. "I don't remember a bunch of girls having a thing for me."

"Then you have a terrible memory," she teased. "Just because you chose not to date in high school doesn't mean there weren't options. You had plenty. Frankly, I got tired of girls constantly bugging me to get to you. I considered circulating a rumor that you were gay just so they'd back off."

"You poor thing," he teased right back. "And how do you think it felt for me to watch all those guys falling all over you, knowing you didn't even see me standing beside you?"

She sobered. She'd seen him. She'd just taken him for granted. Somehow she'd figured he was her backup plan. One of those casual ideas you have in the back of your mind for later. Much later. She chuckled softly at herself for being a blind fool "Well, live and learn, right?"

If she could do it all over again… No, there was no sense going down that road. They'd both made their choices and they had to live with them. She forced a bright smile. "So, what's next? Lunch at The Barbecue Pit? I haven't eaten short ribs in so long I've forgotten how good they are."

"Sure," he murmured, but his hand had drifted to her face. He ran his knuckles along her cheekbones, and she gazed at him, wondering what he was thinking. She didn't have to wait long.

He drew a deep breath as if he needed courage. "Being in love with someone who doesn't feel the same is hard to deal with," he admitted. "And then when they change into someone you don't recognize…I don't know, I couldn't handle it."

Was he apologizing for the way things ended between them so many years ago? She shifted away from him, uncomfortable with the memories that popped up at his admission. She had plenty to apologize for, not him. "It's history," she murmured, not wanting to go further down this road, but he wasn't ready to let it go.

"It's part of *our* history and I have to say this," he said. "You know that day I came to your apartment…"

She remembered it quite clearly. She'd been up for

days, partying hard and fast with a group of friends that she'd picked up at Boston University. "Yeah, you were coming up to visit so I could show you around campus but I called and canceled because I wasn't feeling well," she recalled, but that wasn't the whole truth. She'd been strung out and hadn't wanted to see the disapproval in Tommy's eyes. It probably would've been fine if it hadn't been the third time she'd canceled on him.

"I was worried about you," he said. "But I was a little mad, too. I was tired of taking a backseat to everything else in your life, so I drove to Boston with the intention of doing the one thing I hadn't had the balls to do in high school."

Her brow pulled in a frown. "Which was?"

He leaned forward. "To finally ask you out on a date. To put myself out there and tell you what I'd always felt but was too afraid to say."

"Oh." The word came out in a painful whisper. Knowing that made her feel worse, given what had happened. "I'm sorry," she said.

He shook his head. "You don't need to apologize. I busted in there with my veins full of testosterone. I started it as much as you did."

She blinked back tears that he would be willing to shoulder her burden like that but she knew the true score. "Tommy, I was screwing up. Everything you said was true. I was just too much of a mess to realize it until it was too late and by then I was too ashamed to tell you I was sorry."

His rueful smile warmed her heart even though it felt as if it was cracking. "Seems we both held on to an apology that was way overdue."

"So now what?" she asked. "Where are we now, Tommy?"

He sighed. "I don't know. You said some things that made a lot of sense last night. I don't think I'll ever shake you out of my system. You're like a brand on my soul and as romantic as that sounds, it kinda hurts, too."

At that, she offered a watery smile. "I know what you mean. That's how I feel about you."

"I guess what I'm trying to say is I'm torn between wanting you with me because I love you and always have and pushing you away because I don't know how to forgive and forget. I've never been that kind of man."

"I know."

He caught her gaze. "So I don't know where that leaves us."

"I don't, either." Lord, wasn't that the truth? "But here's the thing…right now we don't have the luxury of figuring it out. I'm not naive, Tommy. I know I've screwed up and there's a possibility that I might see some time for the thefts if restitution isn't enough. And if that happens, our history will remain simply our past. So, let's just take each day as it comes, okay?"

The pain and regret reflecting in his eyes were surely a mirror of her own. She got it. She understood. But sometimes, ignorance was bliss.

The rain started, tapping insistently on the roof of the car, replacing the quiet with its song. Cassi glanced at Tommy, a tiny smile on her lips for the question in her mind.

"So if we could rewrite history, and when you came to me that day in Boston and you'd said your piece and I'd said yes, where would you've taken me?" Tommy didn't seem to want to play this game, but she insisted. "C'mon, where's the harm in seeing what might've happened?"

"Because it hurts, Cassi," he answered darkly. "I've already spent years playing the 'what-if' game and each time it left me with a sense of loss and sadness that I got tired of packing around."

"I understand. I did the same thing, except playing the 'what-if' game and coming up with a better version of what actually happened was the only thing that got me through some really bad times. Who cares if it's total fantasy? It was my lifeline."

He shot her a bemused look. "Really?"

"Yeah," she admitted softly.

He exhaled and his stare dropped to his booted feet as he shifted them for a better position. "Okay," he said, giving in. She smiled as he began, slowly at first as if he were struggling to remember what his plan had been. "Well, let's see… Okay, I'd planned to take you to dinner. I'd scoped out this little place called Bacon, Beans and Beer—"

"Classy. I like it already," she interjected with a teasing grin, and he actually cracked a smile.

"Yeah, well, I was in my twenties. Any place with the word *beer* in the name seemed all right with me."

"As it should."

He laughed, the sound tickling her stomach. "Okay, so this place was supposed to have the best burgers around and I remember you always complaining about the fancy food your mom made you eat so I figured you'd appreciate a good ol'-fashioned burger and fries."

She nodded her approval. "Good choice. Okay, so after we'd stuffed our faces with burgers, what next?"

"A movie?" he answered uncertainly, giving away that either he'd forgotten his plans or he'd planned to wing it. But then, he said a bit sheepishly, "Actually, I'd planned to take you to a club to go dancing."

"You hate to dance."

"I know, but you love to dance, so I thought with enough beer…I'd find my dancing feet, too."

She couldn't help herself and busted up laughing,

causing his cheeks to color. "I'm sorry. I'm not laughing at you...I just think it's adorable that you were prepared to suffer through a night at a club for me. That's awesome. And so are you," she ended with a soft chuckle, wanting so badly to lean over and kiss him. But she didn't. She sobered as the moment faded and she realized what Tommy had meant when he said he didn't like to do this very often. A sharp pain pierced her chest as regret settled heavily on her shoulders. Why hadn't she made better choices? She'd give anything to rewrite that day so that everything from that moment forward was different. She might've finished college. She might've found a better way to help her mother. She might've...been with Tommy.

Scratch that—she *knew* she'd be with Tommy.

And that hurt most of all.

"Are you ready to go?" she asked.

Sensing the change between them, Tommy nodded and pulled away from the school.

LATER THAT NIGHT, WHILE Cassi chatted with Mama Jo in the living room over hazelnut coffee and cinnamon buns, Thomas took a minute to give Owen a call.

"Hey, buddy," Thomas said as Owen came on the line. "How's the fight against the tree huggers going?"

Owen grunted something uncomplimentary and Thomas grinned. "Keep it legal. I don't want to have to come to California to arrest you or anything."

"Someone ought to arrest the group I'm fighting for committing terrorist acts against a law-abiding citizen who's just trying to make a living. There's one in particular that I want to... And there's this reporter who..." Owen made a noise of frustration before saying, "Oh, forget about it. Talking about it makes my blood pressure rise. What's up with you? Still chasing after something personal?"

"Yeah, you could say that," he said with a sigh, deciding to drop the bomb. "It's Cassi."

"Cassi was the personal problem you were dealing with?" Owen's voice rose with incredulity. "Why didn't you say so in the first place?"

"Yeah. It's a long story but suffice it to say she's in my custody."

"Whoa. That's...uh, well, isn't it a conflict of interest of some sort?"

"Yes, but I've got it under control."

"So what's going on? Is she okay? Last I heard you two were on the outs."

"We were." Shit. He'd thought talking about it with his brother might provide some clarity but he was having a hard time just putting it into words. "She's in a bit of trouble but she may have been framed for some of it. I'm trying to help her prove her innocence."

"Sounds like you're the best person for the job. No one knows Cassi like you do. And if there was ever someone who would have her back, it's you. So what's the problem? I can hear in your voice that something is tripping you up."

"She's different. Changed. She's done some things that I don't believe in. You know…she's not the girl we grew up with."

"Of course not," Owen said roughly. "None of us are the kids we used to be. C'mon, Tommy…you're not trying to hold her to some ridiculous standard that no one could live up to are you? 'Cause I know you're better than that."

Thomas shook his head, wishing he hadn't called Owen. He should've kept this to himself. But it was too late. Owen knew the history between him and Cassi, but he didn't know the new stuff. "She's been on the run for two years, stolen identities and before that she was running with a party crowd, doing drugs and shit. Does that sound like the Cassi we knew?"

"Yeah." Owen's blunt answer caught him off guard.

"What?"

Owen chuckled on the other end and Thomas stiffened. "Listen, Tommy, you loved her so you had blinders on. She was always a wild child. You saw what you wanted to see. And that's not to say that she wasn't a great kid. We all were. But she had her demons, just like the rest of us. My guess is you're judging her against a memory that was an illusion to begin with."

"That's bullshit," he retorted, annoyed that Owen would even try to imply that he was that kind of idiot. "My memory is just fine."

"Yeah?"

"Yeah."

"Well, I'm not going to argue the point over a long-distance telephone line. Just do me a favor, try to remember that people grow and change and sometimes it's for the better, not the worse. Okay?"

"Why'd I call you?" he asked sourly.

Owen gave a hearty laugh. "Because you knew I'd tell it to you straight."

"That's the reason I *shouldn't* have called you," Thomas growled, but he was starting to see Owen's point. Damn it. If that was true that meant he'd been a real sanctimonious jackass. And the realization didn't make him feel all warm and fuzzy inside. "Thanks," he muttered with residual ill humor, but he meant the sentiment.

"No problem," Owen said, then drew in a deep breath as if he were resigning himself to a task he hated. "I have to get going. I have a meeting with the city council and that reporter is bound to be there, salivating at the chance to smear me in the local rag again."

"Play nice," Thomas joked, but added in all seriousness, "I hope it works out in your favor, buddy."

"Thanks. Tell Cassi I said hi."

Thomas said goodbye and the line clicked off.

He considered all that Owen had said and wondered how much he'd changed over the years. The perception he had of himself was that he'd remained the same with the basic core set of values he'd been born with.

But perhaps that wasn't entirely true.

He never thought he'd be comfortable carrying a gun, yet he had excelled in weapons training.

He never imagined he'd want to attach himself permanently to anyone, yet he kept thinking how great it would be if Cassi were his wife and perhaps the mother of his children.

He swallowed involuntarily. *Kids.*

He'd always bucked at the thought of having kids, using the job as his excuse. But he knew plenty of agents who were happily married with a passel of kids running around, happy as clams.

He'd never thought a suburban life was his lot.

Yet…the picture was beginning to have some appeal.

To have someone to share his day with, to share the ups and downs of life in general—he could see the value. And when he pictured children, he saw little girls with Cassi's features. A physical ache made him clutch at his chest as if he were having a heart attack. But what if none of that was possible? Take away the obvious issues with her recent criminal past and there was still emotional baggage to deal with.

And if she got a judge who hoped to make an example out of her? She'd definitely see jail time. She thought just because she wrote down in her little book everyone she'd "borrowed" from then everything would be right as rain when she paid them back. If only it were that easy. He groaned. He'd never been conflicted when it came to the parameters of the law. Not so now. He was ashamed to admit that he hoped Cassi walked so that they could figure out their tangled feelings for one another.

There was a small part of him that worried she was putting on a false front for him to gain his sympathy. But if that was the case, he realized, it was working because he'd walk through fire at this point to protect her.

His head started to pound and he was no closer to a resolution in his mind than he was when he started thinking about it.

He wanted Cassi. Shouldn't that be enough?

The question was rhetorical. And the answer made him feel like a miserable, judgmental fool.

CHAPTER SEVENTEEN

CASSI KNEW SHE SHOULDN'T do it but she was drawn to the house, unable to stop herself even as a subtle tremble in the backs of her knees betrayed her nerves. The bastard was in there…living large on her family's fortune, and yet she was the one on the outside looking in.

She'd talked Mama Jo into letting her borrow her car on the pretense of going to the store for some personal items after Tommy had left to do some work at his office.

She knew it was stupid and she was pushing the envelope on reckless but she hadn't been home for years and she was, quite plainly, homesick.

The expansive colonial plantation-style home loomed over the driveway; its red brick and white sideboards caused her throat to ache as a wave of memories washed over her. Her father had purchased this house when he'd married her mother, entranced by the home's history and elegance. She'd known nothing but love and freedom in her earliest childhood but as a teen her relationship with her mother had soured as she became closer to her father.

She'd been too young to see the cracks in her parents' marriage, the loneliness her mother suffered from the long absences her husband took, ostensibly on business. Cassi had only seen the love shining in her father's eyes when he returned. Of course, she hadn't noticed that the love hadn't been directed toward her mother. But Olivia hadn't been blind and she'd withered into a snappish, nervous and high-strung woman who lived for her committees and service groups while George had flourished in the sunshine of unencumbered adventure.

As Cassi stared wistfully at the beautiful home, she suffered a pang of regret for not being the daughter Olivia had dreamed of having but also for not seeing how she'd abandoned her mother, just like her father had.

"Mom, I'm sorry I didn't do right by you when you were alive but I promise I will see the man who killed you brought to justice," she vowed quietly, hoping her mother heard her and knew that she'd always loved her, even if she hadn't been very good at showing it.

She'd considered pulling around to the horse stables to avoid drawing attention to herself but the thought of sneaking around her own home was something she couldn't abide, not now. So she drove right up the driveway, proclaiming with her actions that Lionel could go to hell and that she wasn't afraid of him.

Cassi drew a deep breath and then stepped to the front door and boldly walked in.

Familiar smells assaulted her and she nearly staggered under their emotional weight. The grand staircase curved gently like the flare of a woman's hip and she smiled even though it hurt to remember.

How many times had she run like a heathen through the house, knocking over expensive things in her haste, dashing up the stairs without a care as to the value of the runner cushioning her steps as she tracked mud from the horse barn into the house? More times than she could count. Her father had always laughed at her exuberance; her mother had been distressed by it.

Off somewhere a grandfather clock chimed the hour and she slowly climbed the stairs to where her bedroom once was. The chances were slim that Lionel had kept the room as it was before she was exiled but she was already technically trespassing so she might as well satisfy every ounce of her curiosity.

She crossed to her room and pushed open the door. Tears pricked her eyes as disappointment followed. What had she expected? Every aspect of her influence or ownership of the room had vanished, replaced with chunky furniture and heavily masculine colors appropriate for a game room. An elk's head stared at her where she'd once kept an antique clock imported from France. A large billiards table dominated the room and there were ashtrays filled with the stubbed remains of cigars littering the tables. How disgusting. The stale smell of smoke and liquor wrinkled her nose and made her angry all over again. He'd defiled her room purposefully with his foul habits and vices. She could only imagine what had gone on in here. The man had likely taken great pleasure in tearing down her things and replacing them with the tacky crap he had in there now.

"My decorating tastes are not to your liking?"

A voice at her back caused her to turn slowly, cool rage blotting out all sense of reason and precaution. "Hello, Lionel," she said, narrowing her stare, wishing she had lasers in her eyes so she could fry him. "And no, I can't say I appreciate your sense of *style*."

Lionel, a good-looking man with his graying temples and easy but cunning smile, simply chuckled. "I've missed our verbal sparring. It's not been the same without you. How have you been, dear stepdaughter of mine?"

She ignored that and chose to go to the billiards table and pick up a ball. With one good toss she could likely bury the heavy thing in his head. She hefted it in her hand, testing the weight. Yes, it was safe to say the eight ball could cave in his rotten head quite nicely. "You're an evil man, Lionel Vissher," she stated with a smile that was as cold as it was insincere.

"Oh?" He lifted one brow. "While we wait for the police to arrive, please share. I'm sure yours is a delightful story."

So smug. She hated him with everything in her. She ought to get out before the cops arrived—she certainly didn't need the added complication—but she was fairly vibrating with rage and she couldn't quite get her feet to obey. Not yet anyway. She wanted to see his expression when she told him how he was going down. "I know you're a parasite who preys on rich women. You look for someone who has recently lost a husband and is vulnerable to your charm and charisma and then after a reasonable time has passed, you slowly poison them to death."

He laughed. "Yes, just as I thought. Delightful. My dear, you truly missed your calling. You have a wild imagination and I'm flattered by your estimation of my talents."

"Only you would find flattery in something so damning. But you see, you screwed up and I'm not the only one who knows it. Remember the two old ladies you paid off to file false charges against me in your old haunt of Virginia Beach? Well, only one died. The other is alive and well and ready to press charges as soon as the FBI discovers the evidence linking you to that private investigator you hired to do your dirty work."

His laughter died away and a cold hard look entered his eyes. "Like I said…your imagination is delightful."

"You know what I find delightful? The thought of you rotting in prison with a very large, very *brutal* man with ambiguous sexual tastes for a cell mate."

His lips thinned and his nostrils flared but he otherwise remained silent until a cool smile flitted to his mouth. "It's been a pleasure. I do believe the police have arrived. I know these meetings are awkward, so let's save ourselves the trouble and avoid it next time."

"Getting rid of me so soon? I heard you were looking for me," she said, taunting him. "Chasing down old friends and dropping business cards with the promise of money if they gave you information. You're despicable."

He affected a wounded expression. "Am I a villain because I care too much for my wayward daughter?"

"*Stepdaughter,* you miserable bastard," she spat. "You're the worst kind of villain because you hide behind false smiles and pretty lies. But I'm wise to you and soon you're going to fall. I promise."

"You poor thing. Still suffering from such rage," he said, shaking his head in pity. "I'd hoped you were off the drugs but I see that's not the case."

She stiffened. "You don't know a thing about my life, so don't pretend to."

He pursed his lips. "I know enough."

A chill chased her backside and she gripped the eight ball tighter. She lifted her chin. "Soon you'll be the one being escorted from my home. Do you hear me, Lionel? *My* home. Not yours. Consider yourself on notice. Things are about to change."

Two officers appeared at the top of the stairs. "What seems to be the trouble?" one asked, looking from Cassi to Lionel.

"No trouble, Officer," Cassi said, secretly breathing a little easier now that the police had arrived, even if they were there to toss her out. For a moment she'd felt true malice rolling off Lionel, as if he'd actually contemplated doing something violent. She rolled the ball into the corner pocket and smiled as she pushed past Lionel, saying sweetly. "I was just leaving."

The officers looked to Lionel and he waved them off. "Just a minor disagreement. Thank you, Officers."

The officers shot each other an annoyed look—

another case of rich folk getting off using the police force as their personal guard—and walked with Cassi outside.

They waited until she drove away and then got in their cars, too.

Cassi held in the tears until she was clear of the driveway and then she let them flow as the need for vengeance burned brighter than ever before. "You bloody bastard," she said from between gritted teeth. "I swear you won't get away with this. I swear it!"

Just seeing him again, dressed in the finest imported clothing, walking the halls of her home with impunity, made her shake with unadulterated wrath. Her hands curled on the steering wheel of Mama Jo's antique Buick and she pictured Lionel's neck in her grip.

When she'd been on the run, it was almost possible to forget how much it had hurt to be cast out. She'd had a purpose and it'd fueled her when she weakened in resolve. But seeing her home again brought everything rushing back until she was drowning in a sea of misery that had been dammed for too long.

The temptation to run away from it all was strong but she couldn't allow Lionel to win. Not after everything she'd been through. She couldn't allow him to get away with killing her mother. It was her job to ensure he paid for what he'd done, not only to her but to the other women, as well.

By the time she returned to Mama Jo's her face was streaked from crying and she felt hollow from the misery that had emptied itself with her tears but there was something else, something stronger left in its wake.

"Is that you, Cassi?" Mama Jo asked, coming from around the corner, wiping her hands on a dish-rag. She took in Cassi's splotched face and the anger radiating around her and shook her head. "Did you find what you were looking for, or should I even ask?"

Cassi nodded. She sure did. She found a plan. She knew what she was going to do. She'd give Tommy every chance to bring Lionel down using the might and muscle of the FBI but if they failed and that scum walked...

Well, he wouldn't walk for long.

"Yeah, I found exactly what I needed, Mama Jo. Thanks for the loan of the car."

"Sure, honey," Mama Jo said, eyeing Cassi with faint concern. "You need anything?"

Cassi smiled. "Nope. I think I'm good."

"All right then..."

Cassi lost her smile as soon as Mama Jo turned her back to return to the kitchen.

Justice would find Lionel Vissher.

One way...or another.

THOMAS HAD SPENT THE DAY overseeing the exhumation of Olivia Nolan. Now that the job was finished and Olivia was on her way back to her final resting place, Thomas felt he could breathe again. He made sure there was a rush put on the tissue and hair samples, and after stopping by a local clothing store to pick up a clean shirt so he didn't have to make the trip back to his place, he headed to Mama Jo's.

He found Cassi sitting on the porch, her feet tucked into a blanket, her expression dull.

"It went well," he offered, certain she'd know what he was talking about. She nodded and pulled the blanket tighter around her. He took a seat beside her. "There's a rush on the samples. I know a few guys in forensics and asked for a personal favor. We might have an answer by tomorrow morning if we're lucky."

Cassi perked up and nodded. "Thanks," she said, her voice rusty and hoarse.

"What's wrong? Are you feeling okay?" he asked, concerned. He went to touch her forehead but she moved away from his touch. He frowned. "What's the matter?"

"I'm fine."

"I don't believe you. Something is wrong. Tell me."

"Tommy, if I wanted to share, I would. Some

things are private and I don't care to share them with everyone."

"I'm not *everyone*," he said, offended that he was somehow lumped in with this nebulous group of strangers. "It's me. And given what we've been through in the past few days, not to mention most of our childhood, I'd say I've earned a better spot than some unknown group of nobodies."

She sighed but didn't respond. Frustration at her stonewalling fueled his movements as he jiggled his keys, not quite sure what to say or do. "Fine. You don't want to talk. But whatever it is...I'm here for you if you need me."

He got up to walk inside and she grabbed his hand. "Thank you, Tommy," she whispered and kissed his palm. Her eyes seemed to glitter with unshed tears, but he wasn't sure, for she let go and returned to staring at the moonlit clouds as they moved across a dark night sky.

Thomas walked into the house, still unsettled by Cassi's mood and went to find Mama Jo. He found her sitting in her favorite chair reading one of those horrid gossip magazines that featured alien babies on the cover. She'd always loved the ridiculous rags, often chortling at the stories or at the very least grinning from ear to ear.

But tonight she seemed troubled, too. In fact, after a few minutes, she laid her magazine down with a loud exhale. "There's something eating at that poor girl. Did you figure out what it was?" she asked, getting right to the point.

"No," he answered truthfully. "She pushed me away, said she didn't want to talk about it."

"I got a bad feeling in my bones, Tommy," she said, worried. "She came back this afternoon with a sadness about her, but it was coated with something dark and dangerous."

"Came back? Came back from where?"

Mama Jo looked nonplussed. "She said she needed some personal things from the store. I let her borrow my car."

He swore under his breath. He was willing to bet his front teeth that she hadn't gone to the store like she said. Which begged the question, where'd she go? There was only one place she'd go without him and come back full of rage.

Home.

She must've seen Lionel.

"Damn it, Cassi," he said, looking away.

"Did I do something wrong in letting her borrow my car?" Mama Jo asked, her brows knitting in concern.

Anger at her deception and her recklessness coursed through his veins. In spite of it, he did a fair job of assuring Mama Jo that all was going to be fine. But the truth was, he was pissed.

Mama Jo excused herself to bed and Thomas bade her good-night. As soon as Mama Jo's door closed he stalked outside.

"What were you thinking?" he asked.

She was pulled from her thoughts, and although she was startled by his sudden reappearance, she didn't try to pretend that she didn't know what he was talking about.

"I don't know. I couldn't help myself. It's been so long since I've been home," she answered with a shrug, not the least bit contrite. "Bastard turned my room into a gaudy game room."

"You could've spooked him," he said from between gritted teeth.

She glared at him. "I sure as hell hope I did. That man deserves a sleepless night or two wondering what's going to happen next. If he doesn't get two winks tonight I'll consider today worth the heartache."

"If he skips town we'll have less of a chance to catch him. We need him feeling fat, dumb and happy so we can catch him easily and quickly," he reminded her, but she didn't care.

"I can't handle the thought of that man living one more second without feeling the need to look over his shoulder in fear. I spent the past two years sleeping with one eye open and it's his turn for all the misery he's heaped on me and the countless others whose lives he ruined!" A tear tracked an angry course down her cheek and she didn't bother wiping it away. "My mother is in the *ground* while he parties and plays like a damn carefree bachelor, spending money he didn't earn and I can't stand it anymore. He's living in my house. Taking what doesn't belong to him and I need to see him pay for it. Do you understand? *I need to see him pay.*"

Her shoulders shook and she dropped her head into her hands as she wept. He hadn't realized the emotional toll it would take on her to return home. It was probably why she'd run so far and so quickly. He took her into his arms and held her until the cries became hoarse whimpers. "He will pay," he said, hoping to God he wasn't making a false promise. "But you have to stay away from him. Don't bait him into bolting. That won't help us."

"I know," she said against his shoulder. "I'm just tired of running, tired of being someone I'm not, and I just want to go home. But I can't, because he's there, and no one I love is around anymore," she said in a tear-choked voice that broke his heart.

He held her tighter. "That's not true. I love you, Cassi. You're not alone. You'll never be alone as long as I'm alive." She sagged against him and the tears started fresh. He heard the pain and the anguish, the fear and loneliness, and all he could do was keep her pressed against him as tight as possible. "Promise me you'll stay away from him. Give me the chance to bring him to justice. Please?"

She sniffed back her tears and buried her head against his shoulder. Her arms tightened around him but she hadn't answered him.

"Cassi? Promise me?"

It was a long moment before she did and Thomas felt cold dread tickle his spine.

"I'll try," she whispered.

And he knew he was running out of time.

Cassie was going to do something dreadful and if she did that…there was no turning back.

He'd lose her forever.

CHAPTER EIGHTEEN

THOMAS MADE THE DRIVE to Pittsburgh early, anxious to see if forensics had anything for him. When he saw a sheet of paper in his in-box, he scooped it up, almost too afraid to read it.

His hands shook as he read the findings.

Hair samples from Olivia Nolan showed toxic levels of arsenic in her system.

"Cassi, you were right," he murmured before going straight to Zell's office. He wasn't surprised to see Zell there as early as him, but he was surprised to see Lionel Vissher standing there with him. "Is this a bad time?" he inquired, giving Lionel a hard look.

Zell turned to Lionel and said, "Thank you for sharing your concerns. We'll look into it right away."

Lionel smiled, his teeth white and perfect. "Much obliged, Director Zell. I just want to put this whole sordid mess behind me. The sooner the better."

"Of course," Zell said, waiting for Lionel to leave before dropping his false smile and turning to

Thomas with an equally annoyed expression. "What did I say about keeping your flight risk under control?" he demanded. "I thought you could handle her, but I guess not. Seems Ms. Nolan paid an unscheduled visit to Mr. Vissher and he wasn't happy about it."

"I suppose not," Thomas agreed amiably, making Zell frown suspiciously. "And she shouldn't have done that."

"Why are you agreeing with me so readily?"

Thomas held up the paper with a grin. "Because we've got the sonofabitch. Forensics found arsenic in Olivia Nolan's hair samples. She was poisoned."

"Yes," Zell said, narrowing his gaze. "According to Mr. Vissher...it was Cassie who poisoned her mother, not him."

"Bullshit," Thomas shot back, shaking his head. "He's running scared. He has to try and deflect the evidence. It was him."

"How do you know?"

"Because I know Cassie," Thomas said.

"Not good enough. What proof do you have it was Vissher that did it? We don't have anything on him. By all accounts he's a model citizen while your *girlfriend* is not."

Thomas jerked. "She's not my girlfriend, sir," he protested.

Zell barked a short, unamused laugh. "You're a

terrible liar, Bristol. The day I handed you the file I could see it in your face that you had it bad for this woman, which was only confirmed when you had her in my office. She's clouding your judgment. I want her brought back in and put into federal lockup until we get this figured out."

"No." The word slipped from his lips before he realized what he was saying. But at Zell's double take and accompanying glare, Thomas knew he hadn't said it only in his head. It was too late. He couldn't take it back. So he stood his ground. Zell had been hell-bent for leather against Cassi from the moment they met and it was time he found out why. "What's going on with you and Lionel Vissher?" he said, throwing it out there and seeing what he caught on the hook.

And he hooked one pissed off superior.

"What are you implying?" Zell asked in a growl.

"You've been harsh with Cassi from day one. You've already admitted that you knew we had a history and yet you gave me the file anyway. You wanted me to bring her in and for some reason you've given Vissher ample opportunity to prove his innocence yet you've practically thrown away the key on Cassi. What gives? And before you answer, let me fill you in on a little something about me...I may be a terrible liar but I'm a helluva investigator and if there's one piece of evidence linking you and Vissher together in any way...I will bury you."

Zell turned an awful shade of milky white and his lips all but disappeared as he pressed them together in an angry clamp. "You have some nerve," he bit out, spittle flying to land in a soggy splotch on the desk. "I ought to fire you right now."

"Do it. And I'll have the Bureau of Professional Standards breathing down your neck so fast you won't know what hit you. Something's rotten in Denmark, Zell, and you seem to be at the heart of it. Cassie stays with me."

He left Zell shaking with rage but Thomas knew he was right. And while it felt good to go toe to toe with his jackass superior, he knew he'd only bought a little time. If Zell was in a conspiracy with Vissher in some way, the two would likely try to discredit him or make Cassie disappear.

And there was also the very real possibility he'd just screwed the pooch and tanked his career by making a wild accusation against his superior. All scenarios put together, Thomas didn't feel comfortable in the least.

He had to get back to Cassie. He wanted to share the news...but at the core, he wanted her in his sight. Suddenly, he was short on trust and looking over his shoulder.

As angry as Zell was, he wouldn't put it past him to chuck something heavy his way.

CASSI LISTENED AS TOMMY shared all he'd found out as well as the unexpected appearance of Lionel in Zell's office. She bit her lip in thought, racking her brain for any possible connection that she might've missed. She came up empty. "As far as I know Lionel doesn't have any pull in the Bureau. I mean, he tries to keep a relatively low profile with the law agencies, for obvious reasons. But to be on the safe side, do you have anyone you trust within the Bureau that you could talk to?"

"Yeah, but I think for the time being I'll just wait and see what Zell's next move is. If my accusations are groundless, maybe it'll just die away, but if they aren't, Zell might get scared and do something stupid, which will only bury him."

"I'm not comfortable with the 'sit and wait' plan," she admitted. "What happens now?"

"Well, I'm going to have to bring you in for some formal questioning as Vissher has named you as a suspect. And they'll have to bring Vissher in, too."

"He's an accomplished liar, Tommy. What if no one believes me and they believe him?"

"That's what evidence is for. Evidence doesn't lie," he said.

"I don't know about that," she said, worried.

"He slipped up somewhere. For one, he probably shouldn't have used arsenic. Of all the poisons, it's the easiest to trace because it lingers for so long. But killers get comfortable with one method and tend to stick with it. The court orders for the exhumation of his previous wives are already in process. Chances are they'll have arsenic in their systems, too."

Cassi grabbed her date book and handed it to Tommy. "Everything I ever found on Lionel Vissher is in this date book," she said.

He accepted the ragged book and turned it over gingerly in his hands, flipping the pages open to peruse the contents. He saw dates and times, notes, phone numbers, even pictures stuffed in the side pockets. "You managed to put this portfolio together while trying to survive?" She nodded and his eyes warmed with pride. She could spend a lifetime staring into those eyes, she realized with a start. She leaned into him and he pulled her tight. "You're amazing," he said, kissing her forehead. "You would've made a great investigator."

"I don't know about that," she said. "I was pretty highly motivated and desperate." And scared. She was terrified right now that Lionel was going to walk, just like he always did. There would be no justice for any of his victims, most importantly her mother. She'd have to bring justice to him. She pulled away and he sensed the change in her.

"Cassi…"

She quieted him with a faint kiss brushed against his lips. "Don't say it," she said.

"I have to," he said, looking into her eyes, searching for some kind of assurance that she couldn't give.

She smiled, though it was painful. "It'll all work out. One way or another. I just know it."

A heavy silence settled between them and Cassi didn't trust herself to break it. Instead, she clung to him and prayed. Though she couldn't rightly say what exactly she was praying for. There was a part of her that burned for retribution and hungered for blood, and it warred with the part of her that was crying for closure and wishing for a new beginning that started with Tommy.

She could only wait and see which prayer was answered.

THOMAS WALKED CASSI TO a holding room where she'd be questioned by another member of the team who didn't have any personal connection to her. Cassi had offered to submit to a lie detector and while it was inadmissible in court, Thomas thought it was a good idea just to go that extra mile to show she had nothing to hide.

Lionel Vissher was also in the building for questioning, but he had not agreed to a lie detector test.

In a surprise turn of events, Zell allowed Thomas to interview Lionel. Thomas wasn't going to look a gift horse in the mouth so he just nodded and headed into the interview room.

Lionel, looking polished and relaxed, though a bit bored, glanced up when Thomas entered the room.

"Can we move this along? I have appointments scheduled in the coming hour," he said, adjusting his cuff with sharp agitated movements. "This is ridiculous. I've already told Director Zell where the investigation should be heading and it's not with me. This is a waste of time."

Thomas dropped the case file to the desk and took a seat opposite Lionel. "Thank you for your cooperation, Mr. Vissher," he said without a scrap of sincerity. It was like reading from a teleprompter, that part. He had to say it. Looked good on the tape for later. "As you well know, some interesting information has come to light regarding your late wife, Olivia Nolan. Cause of death has been changed from natural to poisoning by arsenic. You say you knew this?"

Lionel sighed. "Yes. Unfortunately, I was trying to protect my stepdaughter, Cassandra. She's a misguided girl, who always had a hatred for her mother. I figured there'd been enough tragedy—why compound matters with an investigation? It would've mortified my beloved Olivia."

Thomas smirked at the false concern. "Well, that's not your call to make, Mr. Vissher. If you believed your stepdaughter was responsible for your wife's death, it was your civic duty to report her."

"Of course. I am guilty of caring too much, I suppose."

"Yes. Well, let's leave that for the time being and move on to your life before you made Ms. Nolan's acquaintance. Such as…when you were married to Penelope Hogue."

At the mention of his first wife, Lionel actually stiffened and a flash of grief passed over his expression that Thomas believed to be genuine. That was unexpected. Lionel drew a deep breath before answering. "She died of cancer. What of her?"

He pulled a separate file. "You received a decent life insurance payout, didn't you?"

"Which was used to pay her enormous medical bills. What is your point?"

Thomas waved away his question. "Give me a minute…I'll come back to that. Let's go to your next wife…"

"Olivia…"

"No," Thomas shook his head, then met his stare head-on. "I'm talking about Sylvia Williams in Raleigh, North Carolina."

"I don't know who you're talking about."

"No?" He pulled a photo that Cassi had stuffed in

her date book of Lionel, his face in profile, clearly avoiding the camera but caught nonetheless, standing with a stately brunette at some ritzy function. "This isn't you? Sure looks like you. It's odd because she died of the same kind of unexplained ailment as Olivia."

Lionel smiled. "I assure you I don't know this poor woman."

"No? Hmm, how about Lydia Proctor from Virginia Beach? Does that name ring a bell? Surely this one is more recent so it should jog your memory a bit. No? How about a picture?" He produced a photo of Lydia and Lionel smiling, though as usual Lionel was turning his face away from the camera's lens.

Lionel swallowed and paled a bit but admitted to nothing.

Thomas leaned back in the chair. "Here's what I know—all three ladies were slowly poisoned by arsenic. You want to know what else was similar? All three were wealthy ladies with very little family. They were lonely, rich and vulnerable to predators looking for an easy mark. And with each death, the payouts were larger and more substantial."

"Fascinating."

"Yes, isn't it? But there's more. You see, whoever killed these women also killed another using contaminated fruit bars sent as a gift for doing 'the right thing' to help put away a dangerous woman.

Except one of the women didn't die. She's alive and cooperating quite nicely. You see, she feels terrible about her part in all this and she's singing like a bird. And isn't it interesting that when we pulled your financials you had two sizable withdrawals in the exact amounts that were given to the women who filed false reports on Cassandra Nolan? But loose ends are messy, hence the poisoned fruit bars. Not very smart, but it'd worked in the past and who would care about two little old ladies living in a trailer park on a fixed income, right?"

Lionel looked ill but he remained silent.

"Here's what I think—when you lost your first wife it was to natural causes and the insurance payout was nice. Although, like you said, a lot of it went to pay for the medical bills, but it sparked an idea and a hunger for more. You're a good-looking guy, probably never had a problem catching the ladies' eye, so how about finding a sugar mama to help fund your expensive tastes? Except sugar mamas get demanding and you don't like to be tied down. Bye-bye, Sugar Mama. Hello, unencumbered cash flow."

"Interesting theory. Prove it." Lionel stood and Thomas followed.

"I believe I just did," he said, leaning toward Lionel. "You're going to prison, you sonofabitch."

"Let's pretend for a moment that you may be

right, which you're not, but even if you were, the evidence you have is circumstantial. I hardly think that's enough to go to court with."

Thomas smiled, ceding the point. "Perhaps. But it's enough to file charges and due to the unique nature of the case, it's enough to go to trial. And these facts are pretty damning, particularly when we bring the families of your former wives to testify. Seems they found it pretty odd that you just dropped off the face of the planet as soon as the ink dried on the check."

"We all grieve in different ways," he said stiffly.

"True. I bet it's a lot easier to lament the loss of a wife when you're on the prowl for the next one."

"You're rude and offensive," Lionel stated, his lips thinning. "I'm through with this harassment. I expect to take this up with your superior."

"Be my guest. In the meantime, we're taking you into custody on formal murder charges."

"I want to call my lawyer," Lionel said, his mouth trembling, with rage or fear, Thomas wasn't sure. "It's a travesty that I did what I could to protect Cassandra and instead I'm being vilified with circumstantial evidence."

"Save it for the judge," Thomas said, motioning to the agents observing the interview. "Get him out of my sight."

Two agents entered the room and gathered Lionel,

who had begun to struggle but they had no problem subduing him.

"This is preposterous," he thundered as they dragged him from the room. "I'll have your job for this, Agent Bristol. Mark my words, I'll have your head! You can't do this to me!"

"I can and I did." And it felt good.

CHAPTER NINETEEN

THOMAS RETURNED TO MAMA JO'S to tell Cassi the good news in person. He wanted to see the joy in her face when he told her she could stop running and that she could start over.

But as he was on his way he got a call from Zell.

"Listen, I wanted to give you a heads-up…Vissher managed to get his lawyer to convince the judge to let him walk on his own recog until the arraignment."

Thomas swore. "He's going to run," he said.

"He might. We've got the airports and his passport flagged. If he tries, it'll only seal the deal in the case against him."

Thomas wasn't worried about the case. He was worried about Cassi. She wasn't going to take this news lightly.

"Bristol, one more thing," Zell said, his voice roughening. "I'm going to let your allegations slide because you're a good investigator and you were going where you thought the leads took you, but if you ever make an allegation against me like that again…I'll fire your ass. Got it?"

"Yes, sir." He should've left it at that, but he couldn't. He'd never seen Zell act so cagey. "So, mind sharing what was going on with you?"

Zell hesitated, clearly not in the mood, but after a heavy pause he said, "I was getting pressure from higher up to close this case. Resources are needed elsewhere and Ms. Nolan looked good for the suspect at first glance. Not to mention, until you brought different evidence to light…we had no reason to believe Vissher was anything but what he appeared. I don't like that you questioned my behavior but in hindsight I'm glad you didn't let it go. You're a good agent. But don't let it go to your head. I mean it, Bristol. You go berserk on me again and I'll—"

"I get it," he assured Zell. He didn't think he'd need to go this route again. At least he hoped not.

The line went dead and he figured that went as well as it could've, given all that he'd said. But he didn't regret it. He was doing what he felt was right and he'd never apologize for that.

He got to the house and Cassi was there, waiting anxiously. He started with the good news first, saying, "We got him, Cassi. He's been formally charged," he said, taking a moment to enjoy her relieved smile because he knew it wouldn't last. "But

Lionel has already managed to convince the judge to let him walk until the arraignment."

Cassi stepped away from him, hurt in her eyes. "Why? He's clearly guilty. There's a mountain of evidence against him! If he were a regular person without any money do you think he'd get this kind of special treatment?"

"Of course not. Money talks. I'm not going to pretend that that doesn't happen, but the good thing that we have to remember is that he's caught. His passport has been flagged and there's a *Be on the lookout* for him at every law enforcement agency, should he try and bail."

Cassi turned away. "You don't understand how easy it is to disappear with the right resources. I did it with barely two pennies to rub together. Imagine how far Lionel could get with the money at his disposal."

"Well, he doesn't have much to rub together at the moment," Thomas said.

"What do you mean?"

"We froze his assets. It's routine when we believe there's been some kind of fraud. The insurance companies are going to want to go over his financials with a fine-tooth comb. Trust me, his standard of living is going to change dramatically, and if he runs he's going to learn quickly how hard life is without a penny to your name."

"Yeah, but knowing Lionel, he has cash stashed away, too. Trust me, he's got resources." Cassi said with a hard light in her eyes that made him nervous.

"I know what you're thinking."

"Do you?"

"Yes. You're thinking that he's getting away with killing your mother. That once again he's escaped justice. That's not what has happened."

"Feels like it."

"There's a process and *it will work*. But you've gotta give it a chance and don't screw it up by doing something rash. You can't bring your mom back no matter what you do."

She stepped away from him. "I know that. But I can avenge her."

He followed her quickly, grasping her arms. "Yes, you can...by living and doing your part to see him put away for his crimes. Your mom would've wanted you to be happy, not sitting in prison because you were consumed with revenge. Take a chance on life. Take it with me."

She startled and drew a sharp breath at his plea. What was he asking? "I don't understand...we don't have a future, Tommy. I have a record. Even if none of the other charges stick...I don't fit in with your life now. We'd be fools to think that I could."

"I don't care about that other stuff. All I want is you. No matter how you come to me."

Tears blinded her. He was asking her to turn away from her need for vengeance in return for a life with him. It was an illusion, the two of them riding off into the sunset. No matter how she might want it, it was futile to chase after a dream that was bound to die.

"I can't."

"You can't…or you won't?"

"Tommy," she cried. "It's not as simple as you make it sound. I'm not the person I used to be. I'm not the person you want me to be. I'm not the person you want to be tied down to. Trust me on this before we both hurt each other irrevocably with our failure. I'd rather preserve what we had than try to patch together something new and fail."

"I know who you are," Tommy insisted, refusing to back down. "I knew the minute I opened that file what I was getting into, and I couldn't fathom letting anyone else handle this case. I know what you've done and I don't care. It's not who you are. Circumstances change us, you're right, but they don't define us unless we let them. I want you—flaws and all—because you've always been the one. And nothing has changed that. Nothing." He pulled her to him and she went, tears streaming down her face.

"Nothing will change that," he murmured against her lips. "I love you."

What she heard was Tommy asking her to pick him. To love him more than she hated Lionel. And she did. She loved him so much it hurt to breathe at the thought of walking away from him again.

She was afraid of failing him, of failing herself. "I'm so scared," she murmured.

"Me, too," he admitted, pressing his forehead to hers, holding her gently. "But we can do this. Together."

Together. A great shudder traveled through her body at the word.

The love of her life.

Even if it meant letting her hatred for Lionel go.

She wanted to—she just didn't know if she was capable. The anger inside her demanded action. She knew, deep in her heart, she would only be able to ignore it for so long before she got restless and did something reckless, like disappear to chase after him and that would crush Tommy. She couldn't do that to him. She pulled away, her eyes brimming. "I can't make that promise. Not yet. I'm sorry."

"Cassi." His voice was colored with exasperation and perhaps, fear. "Don't do this. You have a choice. You can choose to walk away from all that crap in your past and start over. Not many people are given that chance. Don't blow it over your need for revenge."

"Don't lecture me on what the right thing to do is. You don't know what kind of hell I've been through."

"No, but I know what it's like to go through hell and come out the other side feeling like a chewed-up piece of meat. Mama Jo gave me the chance to start over and I'm giving you that opportunity. Don't you want to start over?" he asked, his voice plaintive.

"Of course I do, but let's get real. What kind of life am I looking at? It's not like I can just slide back into my old life like slipping on an old shoe. I'm different! And, there are things about myself that I don't want to change! I'm strong, much stronger than I ever was when I lived here," she said, but her lip trembled. "I'm restless from being on the run. I get antsy when I'm in one place too long and I—"

"Stop, Cassi," he demanded. "You're throwing everything but the kitchen sink in with your reasons why you can't do this with me, but I'm not stupid. It has everything to do with your damn need for vengeance, so stop trying to bolster it with anything other than the ugly truth."

"Fine," she shot back, tears leaking from her eyes. "It's about vengeance. I want to see him burn for what he did. I want to know that he's getting reamed every day of his life for taking so much from me. My mother died thinking I hated her! She died thinking I was...*bad*." She choked on the word. "She died alone and I couldn't do a thing to help her. You don't understand what that feels like and you can't tell me that I shouldn't demand his head on a stick because it's not *the socially acceptable thing to do*."

His features darkened and every muscle in his body tensed as he seemed to tower over her. Control was evident in the rigid posture of his shoulders but there was fury in his eyes. "You are not the only one who has ever lost a loved one, Cassi. You did not corner the market on grief," he snarled, causing her to falter but she held her ground. "Everyone has a sob story somewhere in their life. Maybe their uncle touched them in a bad way, maybe their mother was an alcoholic and used to beat them, or maybe—" his voice rose to a roar "—just maybe their father went on a bender and blew his whole damn family to hell one night because he imagined that his wife was cheating on him! So don't whine to me that you're the only one who's ever been given a bad hand, because it's bullshit and I'm not going to listen."

She opened her mouth but nothing came out except a strangled sob. Her chest hurt. It felt as if someone had heaved their foot through her rib cage and it was stuck on one of her internal organs.

Tommy turned and jerked his hand in a gesture

that said "do what you want" and growled as he walked away, "Whatever, Cassi...I put myself out there but you're not interested. You're going to do what you want anyway, but just remember this... if you break the law, I will come for you and this time...I *won't* have your back."

THOMAS WANTED TO BREAK THINGS. He strode past Mama Jo on the laundry porch as he headed for the backyard. She paused in folding her towels, noting his thunderous expression and simply said, "There's some logs out back that could use splitting. Go ahead and put that piss and vinegar to good use before you blow your top off."

Mama Jo had always maintained that anger was an emotion that needed to move out physically or else it just hung around in your heart, waiting for an opportunity to raise its ugly head. So when the boys got riled up, she'd send them out to split logs.

Sending a maul through a stubborn piece of knotty oak was backbreaking work and it did the trick. By the time they were finished, they were exhausted and couldn't quite work up a puff of smoke much less a whistle of steam.

And that's exactly what he needed. He was so mad with Cassi he didn't trust himself and he knew he needed time to cool off.

He grabbed the splitting maul and muscled the

first log into place, grunting with the exertion, his breath pluming in the cold, then sent the maul slicing into the hard wood with a satisfying thunk that reverberated through his arm and up his shoulder. He yanked it free and sent it sailing again until the wood cracked and broke off in chunks.

And then he started again.

About an hour later, sweat raining down his face, he looked up to see Mama Jo, ostensibly coming out to check his progress. He felt a lecture coming on and he wasn't in the mood. "Mama, just leave me be. I gotta work this out on my own."

"Of course you do," she agreed. "You're a full-grown man. What's to say that you don't already know?"

He paused to give her a speculative stare. "What does that mean?" he asked.

She raised her hands, weathered and careworn from soothing so many young brows, including his own, and simply shrugged. "I'm just saying, you already know what needs to be done. I only came out to see how you're doing with those logs. Watch yourself, now. You don't want to pull a muscle."

His mouth firmed. "Thanks. You ought to get inside. You'll catch a cold or something out there."

She leveled a short stare his way that made him feel fifteen again. "I'm a long ways away from taking orders from you, Thomas Bristol. Don't you worry none about me. I'm tougher than a fighting rooster."

This was true, Thomas thought. "All right, suit yourself. Just don't try and lecture me on Cassi. My temper is too hot."

"Sure. I understand. Love will do that to you, I know." Love. He felt an overwhelming urge to spit on the ground but refrained for Mama's sake. She continued as if she hadn't noticed his grunt of annoyance. Sighing, she said, "Do you remember how you felt when you came here?"

"Mama—"

"Just answer the question, please."

He gritted his teeth but answered just the same. "Pissed off, scared, lonely. Take your pick. You remember what I was like. You tell me."

"Yes, all those and more. But mostly, broken-hearted. The anger is easy to get through. It's mending the broken parts that's the hardest. And even if you manage to put everything back the way it was, it'll always be fragile, always in danger of breaking again."

"I know that, Mama," he said bitterly. It's why he couldn't bear to look at old pictures of his family. He was afraid seeing them again would cause him to shatter inside, when he'd worked so hard at putting everything back together again.

"If you know it then why is it so hard for you to

see that there are broken parts inside Cassi, too? She needs your help, not your anger."

"I tried." He turned away and hefted the maul. "You can't help someone who doesn't want the help. Just a fact of life, Mama."

"You gave her an ultimatum."

He sent the maul whistling into the log, burying it. He looked at Mama, pain roughing his voice, as he said, "I gave her my heart." He jerked the maul free. "And she threw it on the ground. End of story. I was a fool to think anything could be different, given our history."

He tossed the maul and gathered the wood to start stacking. He was done talking and Mama knew it.

She turned to leave but just as she reached the back door, she said, "Tommy, I've had the privilege of raising you and seeing you turn into a fine adult. You've given me all sorts of reasons to be proud of the way you've turned out but right now, you're being a stubborn, pigheaded fool who's about to lose the one person in this world who ever had the power to truly heal those broken spots in your heart. I can't believe how disappointed I am in you right this minute. You'd rather stand here alone in your fury than help a woman who needs you no matter what she might say. I've said my piece and that's all I'm gonna say. Make sure you put the tarp over the wood, if you please, when you're finished." She ended with a dark scowl before disappearing into the house.

"Damn it!" he swore under his breath, his chest laboring for air from the work out in the chill temperatures. "Sonofabitch!"

Mama's strident tone reached him from inside the house. "I can hear you and I still have soap I can stick in your mouth."

Ah, hell. He rubbed the back of his neck and then wiped the sweat with his forearm. Was Mama right? He had a sinking feeling that she was. But even if that was so, what was he supposed to do about it?

CHAPTER TWENTY

TEARS BLINDED HER BUT SHE made her way to the road, where she managed to hitch a ride. She didn't look back but then she didn't expect Tommy to run after her, either.

Her feelings were so tangled she didn't know if that was what she wanted or not.

She got the driver to drop her off at the gated entrance of her old home and she walked the rest of the way.

She fished her key from her purse and let herself in, surprised that Lionel hadn't changed the locks. The smug bastard had probably felt pretty secure in the belief that she wouldn't return.

The house was an empty shell; the hired help were long gone for the day and seeing as Lionel was probably trying to skip the country, she didn't fear his sudden appearance. Not that he'd scare her anyway. Lionel wasn't the type to get his hands dirty.

There wasn't much of her mother left in the house, she realized, going room to room, noting the differences. Lionel had changed the decor from her mother's favored French provincial to more masculine accents. The furniture was chunky and solid, whereas her mother had loved the spindly-legged antiques she'd often searched Europe for. She had particularly loved when she'd found a piece with genuine royal history. Funny, Cassi hadn't cared for the style when she'd lived at home, but now she missed it. She peered out the window and saw the dark shape of the stables. At least he hadn't gotten rid of the horses. Perhaps because he'd fancied himself a man with fine tastes and that required a certain knowledge or at least possession of horseflesh in these parts.

After a thorough tour, she realized any trace of what had made this her home had been replaced. Her mother's spirit had flown along with her furnishings, and the energy of the house had completely changed.

What would she do with it? Sell it? She exhaled, not quite sure. Her father had loved this house. Well, she supposed she had some time to figure it out.

She turned and nearly screamed as a silhouette in the darkened foyer stood watching her.

She knew it wasn't Tommy.

Lionel stepped forward, his expression menacing. "Cassandra…you've made things difficult and for the life of me, I can't figure out what happened. Perhaps you can shed some light on the situation."

She moved away, keeping a healthy distance between them. "That's easy," she answered evenly. "You're a pathetic predator who preys on women and I managed to find enough evidence of your sloppy work to put you away. Yay me. Does that about sum it up?"

An ugly smile lit up his face as he advanced. "So smart," he sneered. "Wrapped everything up nice and tidy with a cute little bow, didn't you?"

"Well, I wouldn't go that far, but I seem to have accomplished my goal. You're going to go away for a long time and I won't lose a minute of sleep over it." She skirted a large coffee table. "Tell me, what exactly is your plan now? You can't seriously think that it was smart to come here when you're a wanted man? I figured you'd be long gone since you managed to convince the judge to let you walk for the time being. Now you get to find out what it feels like to be hunted."

He didn't appear worried. "I'm not going to prison."

"That's news to the people who are going to put you away, such as the feds," she countered, sweat starting to bead her forehead. "But just for the sake of argument, what makes you think you're going to get away with murder?"

"I have a plane waiting for me and enough money to disappear. I'd considered toughing it out—the evidence is purely circumstantial—but I couldn't take the risk that an unsympathetic jury might not see things my way. Besides, Bridgeport was beginning to bore me anyway. As is being single. Time to find a new special lady to spend some quality time with," he answered, getting closer, and she was running out of places to maneuver. He smiled again. "But first, I have some unfinished business. A loose end, if you will, that needs tying up."

She had a good idea of what—or who—that loose end was, and she tensed, her stare darting to the nearest exit. "Yeah?" she said, almost conversationally, though fear had begun to seep through her pores. "So what? You're going to kill me?"

"The thought has some appeal. You know I could've done it years ago but I figured you were making enough trouble for yourself that I didn't need to bother."

She twisted her mouth derisively. "Sorry to disappoint. It's one of my worst habits."

He shrugged. "Live and learn. Now, would you be a dear and be still. I'm going to enjoy killing you." He pulled a gun from his back waistband and popped off a shot just as she dived behind a sofa. A puff of stuffing erupted from the bullet and Cassi swallowed a gasp as she heard the shot embed in the wood only inches from her chest. Thank God for the ugly, manly furniture. Her mother's furniture wouldn't have stopped a BB pellet much less a .32 caliber.

As she crawled on her belly, getting ready to make a run for the next room, she wished she hadn't been so quick to push Tommy away. Right about now, she could use a little muscle.

TOMMY HEARD THE SHOT JUST as he stepped onto the landing of Cassi's former home. Adrenaline spiking, he returned to his car and unlocked the glove box to retrieve his Glock. He also radioed for backup to the local police then, sticking to the shadows, managed to quietly enter the house. He could hear voices. Cassi and Visscher. He swore softly. He hadn't taken the man for suicidal. Why would he come back? Only one reason Thomas could figure and that was to wipe out a troublesome loose end. *Cassi.*

CASSI SPRUNG FROM HER position and another shot rang out close on her heels. She ran full tilt for the adjoining sitting room and banged her shin on an end table, knocking over a heavy vase in the process. She cringed as it crashed to the floor but wasted little time in one spot. Lionel ran around the corner and fired again—this time the bullet embedded itself in the plaster beside her. She quickly shrank back.

Lionel flicked the light on, bathing the room with a soft glow.

"Ah, there you are. Fast on your feet, aren't you?" he said, smiling. "But there's no point in running anymore. I've won this round."

"I wouldn't say that," she said, lifting her chin, her hand closing around a large, palm-size decorative orb. Without warning she lobbed the crystal paperweight straight at Lionel's head, connecting hard and knocking him silly. He staggered, but his grip on the gun didn't weaken. She ran headlong toward him, sending a roundhouse kick straight into his sternum that sent the gun skidding away and then as he tried to recover, she took great pleasure in sending her fist straight into his stunned face. He collapsed to the hardwood floor, bloody drool dribbling down his chin, stone-cold unconscious. She retrieved the gun to stand over him.

"I win, you bastard," Cassi crowed, her chest heaving with exertion and victory. "And you *are* going to prison. That's a damn promise."

THOMAS SAW CASSI, STANDING over Lionel, looking like an avenging angel full of fury and retribution, and he thought she'd never looked more beautiful. She'd been right. She didn't need him to save her. She'd saved herself and he was proud of her.

He stepped into the light, catching Cassi's stare.

He glanced at Lionel's still form and his mouth quirked in a grin as he holstered his weapon. "I bet that felt good," he said.

"You're damn right it did and I'm not sorry."

He lifted his hands in a conciliatory gesture. "No one is asking you to be. Not me at least."

She grinned and he went to the telephone. "May I?" he asked, motioning to the wiring.

"Be my guest," she answered, and he ripped the cords free to secure Lionel while they waited for the cops to arrive. "Did you see everything?" she asked.

"Pretty much."

"And?" she asked, waiting for some kind of disapproval, but she didn't get it.

"And I think I'm thankful you only punched me."

His dry retort caused laughter to bubble up from inside her. She smiled, glancing at him from beneath lowered lashes. "Well, I did tell you I pulled the punch. I have moves you've never even seen," she teased softly.

He laughed. "Of that I have no doubt. However, how about I promise not to act like a sanctimonious jerk and you promise not to take out my manhood with one of your moves?"

She went to him and slid her arms around him. "Deal." They stood forehead to forehead, allowing the moment to fold around them before she spoke again. "I'm sorry," she admitted in a soft voice.

He pulled away so he could meet her gaze. "I'm the one who's sorry. I shouldn't have said those things."

"Some of what you said was right."

"And some of it was totally out of line," he countered.

They were both right. She nodded, accepting his apology just as he accepted hers. "So what now?"

"Now, we deliver this sonofabitch to the authorities, who are on their way as we speak, and then we go get a hotel room and settle in for the night because I am not sleeping alone, it's too far to my apartment and I'm ending this night with your body pressed against mine. We'll figure everything else out in the morning."

"I like the sound of that."

She smiled up at him. For the moment the shadows were gone, but he knew they would return. He knew because there were still days that made him flinch when the memories came back and he suspected it would be the same for her. But this time, when they came, he wanted her to know that he'd be there for her, just as he knew she'd be there for him.

"And one more thing," he said, his expression turning somber and shining with the integrity she'd come to know and expect from Tommy Bristol. "I will always have your back." His hands reached between them to cup and cradle her face as if it were the rarest of gems and held her gaze. *"Always."*

Tears welled in her eyes. That's all she'd ever needed.

It'd just taken a while for her to realize it.

EPILOGUE

CASSI PULLED UP HER PANT LEG and Tommy hesitated.

"Tommy..." Cassi warned but there was laughter in her voice.

"I don't know. I kinda like the idea of being able to find you no matter where you go," he said, gesturing at the GPS anklet.

"A little mystery is good for any relationship," Cassi quipped. "Now take it off before I go insane."

"All right," Tommy said, unlocking the tracking device and tossing it to the waiting agent. "You're free and clear. Aside from informal probation for the theft charges, you're on the path to total law-abiding citizen status. What are you going to do with your newfound freedom and fortune? Thinking of some travel?"

"Actually, I think I've done enough traveling for the time being. Right now I was thinking of doing some home shopping. I want a place I can call my own without any bad memories."

"A fresh start," Tommy said, nodding. "Sounds good. What did you have in mind?"

She smiled coyly. "Oh, something big enough with room to grow but not so big that it feels cavernous. You know, something homey."

"Are you saying my apartment isn't to your liking any longer?" he joked.

"Well, apartment living was never really my style. Besides, your downstairs neighbors have been giving us the evil eye for our nocturnal activities, as they call it."

Tommy laughed, and the sound warmed her heart and tickled her toes, for it was hard to suppress the memories of their "activities."

"So, what are you saying? You want to move out?"

"I'm saying…we're going to need a house of our own when we decide to make it official and tie the knot. Perhaps something near Mama Jo. Oh, and that's another thing, I want to have some repairs done to her place. Maybe splurge on some new furniture for her."

"Good luck with that. She's notoriously stubborn when it comes to those things. I've tried for years to get her to let me pay for a new roof but she always puts me off."

"We'll see," she said, grinning as another thought

came to her. "You know she's having a fit over our living situation. Do you ever plan on making an honest woman out of me?"

At that, Tommy sobered. "Nothing would give me greater pleasure."

She stared at him. "Really?"

"Really. I want to marry you, Cassandra Amelia Nolan. If you'll have me, that is."

His uncertainty was endearing. As if she'd say no. She hadn't wanted to push him but she'd been dreaming of this for a while. Perhaps longer than she realized. And if he was offering…she was going to take it.

She smiled up at him with all the love she felt bursting from her heart and said, "A thousand times yes, Thomas Eric Bristol. Yes!"

Relief flooded his features as she jumped into his arms and he swung her around until she was dizzy. "Thank God," he said, setting her down. "It was going to be really awkward trying to talk you into having my babies otherwise. It might've given Mama Jo a heart attack."

She laughed. "We can't have that. We're going to need her. Neither one of us knows a thing about raising kids!"

"You got that right," he agreed, but as he nuzzled

her neck, he added, "But it's going to be lots of fun trying to figure it out."

"You got that right," she murmured, gazing up at him. "And I can't wait."

* * * * *

Mama Jo's boys are all grown-up now.
Thomas found his happy ending,
but Christian Holt has his hands full
when he meets Skye D'Lane.
Will he get his happy ending, too?
Be sure to find out in
A CHANCE IN THE NIGHT,
the second book in the
MAMA JO'S BOYS trilogy
by Kimberly Van Meter.

COMING NEXT MONTH

Available April 12, 2011

#1698 RETURN TO THE BLACK HILLS
Spotlight on Sentinel Pass
Debra Salonen

#1699 THEN THERE WERE THREE
Count on a Cop
Jeanie London

#1700 A CHANCE IN THE NIGHT
Mama Jo's Boys
Kimberly Van Meter

#1701 A SCORE TO SETTLE
Project Justice
Kara Lennox

#1702 BURNING AMBITION
The Texas Firefighters
Amy Knupp

#1703 DESERVING OF LUKE
Going Back
Tracy Wolff

You can find more information on upcoming
Harlequin® titles, free excerpts and more at
www.HarlequinInsideRomance.com.

REQUEST YOUR FREE BOOKS!
2 FREE NOVELS PLUS 2 FREE GIFTS!

Harlequin®

Super Romance®

Exciting, emotional, unexpected!

YES! Please send me 2 FREE Harlequin® Superromance® novels and my 2 FREE gifts (gifts are worth about $10). After receiving them, if I don't wish to receive any more books, I can return the shipping statement marked "cancel." If I don't cancel, I will receive 6 brand-new novels every month and be billed just $4.69 per book in the U.S. or $5.24 per book in Canada. That's a saving of at least 15% off the cover price! It's quite a bargain! Shipping and handling is just 50¢ per book in the U.S. and 75¢ per book in Canada.* I understand that accepting the 2 free books and gifts places me under no obligation to buy anything. I can always return a shipment and cancel at any time. Even if I never buy another book, the two free books and gifts are mine to keep forever.

135/336 HDN FC6T

Name	(PLEASE PRINT)

Address	Apt. #

City	State/Prov.	Zip/Postal Code

Signature (if under 18, a parent or guardian must sign)

Mail to the Reader Service:
IN U.S.A.: P.O. Box 1867, Buffalo, NY 14240-1867
IN CANADA: P.O. Box 609, Fort Erie, Ontario L2A 5X3

Not valid for current subscribers to Harlequin Superromance books.
**Are you a current subscriber to Harlequin Superromance books
and want to receive the larger-print edition?
Call 1-800-873-8635 or visit www.ReaderService.com.**

* Terms and prices subject to change without notice. Prices do not include applicable taxes. Sales tax applicable in N.Y. Canadian residents will be charged applicable taxes. Offer not valid in Quebec. This offer is limited to one order per household. All orders subject to credit approval. Credit or debit balances in a customer's account(s) may be offset by any other outstanding balance owed by or to the customer. Please allow 4 to 6 weeks for delivery. Offer available while quantities last.

Your Privacy—The Reader Service is committed to protecting your privacy. Our Privacy Policy is available online at www.ReaderService.com or upon request from the Reader Service.

We make a portion of our mailing list available to reputable third parties that offer products we believe may interest you. If you prefer that we not exchange your name with third parties, or if you wish to clarify or modify your communication preferences, please visit us at www.ReaderService.com/consumerschoice or write to us at Reader Service Preference Service, P.O. Box 9062, Buffalo, NY 14269. Include your complete name and address.

*Selene wanted nothing to do with the father of her son,
Alex; but Aristedes had other plans...that included them.*

*Read on for an sneak peek from
THE SARANTOS SECRET BABY by Olivia Gates,
available April 2011, only from Harlequin Desire.*

"You were right to turn my marriage offer down," Aristedes said.

And Selene found her voice at last, found the words that would not betray the blow he'd dealt her. "Thanks for letting me know. You didn't have to come all the way here, though. You could have just let it go. I left yesterday with the understanding that this case is closed."

Before the hot needles behind her eyes could dissolve into an unforgivable display of stupidity and weakness, she began to close the door.

The door stopped against an immovable object. His flat palm.

"I can't accept that." His voice was low, leashed.

What did her tormentor mean now? Was he ending one game only to start another?

She raised eyes as bruised as her self-respect to his, found nothing there but solemnity and determination.

Before she could voice her confusion, he elaborated. "I never let anything go unless I'm certain it's unworkable. I realize I made you an unworkable offer, and that's why I'm withdrawing it. I'm here to offer something else. A workability study."

She leaned against the door, thankful for its support and partial shield. "Your son and I are not a business venture you can test for feasibility."

His gaze grew deeper, made her feel as if he was trying to delve into her mind, take control of it. "It's actually the other way around. I'm the one who would be tested."

She shook her head. "Why bother? I know—and *you* know—you're not workable. Not with me."

His spectacular eyebrows lowered over eyes she felt were emitting silver hypnosis. "You're right again. Neither you nor I have any reason to believe that isn't the truth. The only truth. It might be best for both you and Alex to never hear from me again, to forget I exist. But then again, maybe not. I'm only asking for the chance for both of us to find out for certain. You believe I'm unworkable in any personal relationship. I've lived my life based on that belief about myself. I never really had reason to question it. But I have one now. In fact, I have two."

Find out what happens in
THE SARANTOS SECRET BABY by Olivia Gates,
available April 2011, only from Harlequin Desire.

SPECIAL EDITION

Life, Love, Family and Top Authors!

In April, Harlequin Special Edition features
four *USA TODAY* bestselling authors!

FORTUNE'S JUST DESSERTS
by MARIE FERRARELLA
Follow the latest drama featuring the ever-powerful
and passionate Fortune family.

YOURS, MINE & OURS
by JENNIFER GREEN
Life can't get any more chaotic for Amanda Scott.
Divorced and a single mom, Amanda had given up on
the knight-in-shining-armor fairy tale until a friendship
with Mike becomes something a little more....

THE BRIDE PLAN (*SECOND-CHANCE BRIDAL* MINISERIES)
by KASEY MICHAELS
Finding love and second chances for others is
second nature for bridal-shop owner Chessie.
But will *she* finally get her second chance?

THE RANCHER'S DANCE
by ALLISON LEIGH
Return to the Double C Ranch this month—where love, loss
and new beginnings set the stage for Allison Leigh's latest title.

*Look for these titles and others in April 2011
from Harlequin Special Edition, wherever books are sold.*

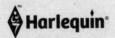

Harlequin®

A *Romance* FOR EVERY MOOD™

www.eHarlequin.com

SEUSA0411

Harlequin Romance

MARGARET WAY

In the Australian Billionaire's Arms

Handsome billionaire David Wainwright isn't about to let
his favorite uncle be taken for all he's worth by mysterious
and undeniably attractive florist Sonya Erickson.

But David soon discovers that Sonya's no greedy
gold digger. And as sparks sizzle between them, will
the rugged Australian embrace the secrets of her past
so they can have a chance at a future together?

*Don't miss this incredible new tale,
available in April 2011
wherever books are sold!*

Harlequin

A *Romance* FOR EVERY MOOD™

www.eHarlequin.com

HRI7722

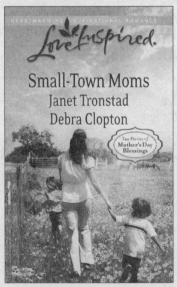